The
River's End

A New Story of God's Country

By James Oliver Curwood

The River's End

Table of Contents

CHAPTER 1

Between Conniston, of His Majesty's Royal Northwest Mounted Police, and Keith, the outlaw, there was a striking physical and facial resemblance. Both had observed it, of course. It gave them a sort of confidence in each other. Between them it hovered in a subtle and unanalyzed presence that was constantly suggesting to Conniston a line of action that would have made him a traitor to his oath of duty. For nearly a month he had crushed down the whispered temptings of this thing between them. He represented the law. He was the law. For twenty-seven months he had followed Keith, and always there had been in his mind that parting injunction of the splendid service of which he was a part—"Don't come back until you get your man, dead or alive." Otherwise—

A racking cough split in upon his thoughts. He sat up on the edge of the cot, and at the gasping cry of pain that came with the red stain of blood on his lips Keith went to him and with a strong arm supported his shoulders. He said nothing, and after a moment Conniston wiped the stain away and laughed softly, even before the shadow of pain had faded from his eyes. One of his hands rested on a wrist that still bore the ring-mark of a handcuff. The sight of it brought him back to grim reality. After all, fate was playing whimsically as well as tragically with their destinies.

"Thanks, old top," he said. "Thanks."

His fingers closed over the manacle-marked wrist.

Over their heads the arctic storm was crashing in a mighty fury, as if striving to beat down the little cabin that had dared to rear itself in the dun-gray emptiness at the top of the world, eight hundred miles from civilization. There were curious waitings, strange screeching sounds, and heart-breaking meanings in its strife, and when at last its passion died away and there followed a strange quiet, the two men could feel the frozen earth under their feet shiver with the rumbling reverberations of the crashing and breaking fields of ice out in Hudson's Bay. With it came a dull and steady roar, like the incessant rumble of a far battle, broken now and then—when an ice mountain split asunder—with a report like that of a sixteen-inch gun. Down through the Roes Welcome into Hudson's Bay countless billions of tons of ice were rending their way like Hunnish armies in the break-up.

"You'd better lie down," suggested Keith.

Conniston, instead, rose slowly to his feet and went to a table on which a seal-oil lamp was burning. He swayed a little as he walked. He sat down,

5

and Keith seated himself opposite him. Between them lay a worn deck of cards. As Conniston fumbled them in his fingers, he looked straight across at Keith and grinned.

"It's queer, devilish queer," he said.

"Don't you think so, Keith?" He was an Englishman, and his blue eyes shone with a grim, cold humor. "And funny," he added.

"Queer, but not funny," partly agreed Keith.

"Yes, it is funny," maintained Conniston. "Just twenty-seven months ago, lacking three days, I was sent out to get you, Keith. I was told to bring you in dead or alive—and at the end of the twenty-sixth month I got you, alive. And as a sporting proposition you deserve a hundred years of life instead of the noose, Keith, for you led me a chase that took me through seven different kinds of hell before I landed you. I froze, and I starved, and I drowned. I haven't seen a white woman's face in eighteen months. It was terrible. But I beat you at last. That's the jolly good part of it, Keith—I beat you and GOT you, and there's the proof of it on your wrists this minute. I won. Do you concede that? You must be fair, old top, because this is the last big game I'll ever play." There was a break, a yearning that was almost plaintive, in his voice.

Keith nodded. "You won," he said.

"You won so square that when the frost got your lung—"

"You didn't take advantage of me," interrupted Conniston. "That's the funny part of it, Keith. That's where the humor comes in. I had you all tied up and scheduled for the hangman when—bing!—along comes a cold snap that bites a corner of my lung, and the tables are turned. And instead of doing to me as I was going to do to you, instead of killing me or making your getaway while I was helpless—Keith—old pal—YOU'VE TRIED TO NURSE ME BACK TO LIFE! Isn't that funny? Could anything be funnier?"

He reached a hand across the table and gripped Keith's. And then, for a few moments, he bowed his head while his body was convulsed by another racking cough. Keith sensed the pain of it in the convulsive clutching of Conniston's fingers about his own. When Conniston raised his face, the red stain was on his lips again.

"You see, I've got it figured out to the day," he went on, wiping away the stain with a cloth already dyed red. "This is Thursday. I won't see another Sunday. It'll come Friday night or some time Saturday. I've seen this frosted lung business a dozen times. Understand? I've got two sure days ahead of me, possibly a third. Then you'll have to dig a hole and bury me.

After that you will no longer be held by the word of honor you gave me when I slipped off your manacles. And I'm asking you—WHAT ARE YOU GOING TO DO?"

In Keith's face were written deeply the lines of suffering and of tragedy. Yesterday they had compared ages.

He was thirty-eight, only a little younger than the man who had run him down and who in the hour of his achievement was dying. They had not put the fact plainly before. It had been a matter of some little embarrassment for Keith, who at another time had found it easier to kill a man than to tell this man that he was going to die. Now that Conniston had measured his own span definitely and with most amazing coolness, a load was lifted from Keith's shoulders. Over the table they looked into each other's eyes, and this time it was Keith's fingers that tightened about Conniston's. They looked like brothers in the sickly glow of the seal-oil lamp.

"What are you going to do?" repeated Conniston.

Keith's face aged even as the dying Englishman stared at him. "I suppose—I'll go back," he said heavily.

"You mean to Coronation Gulf? You'll return to that stinking mess of Eskimo igloos? If you do, you'll go mad!"

"I expect to," said Keith. "But it's the only thing left. You know that. You of all men must know how they've hunted me. If I went south—"

It was Conniston's turn to nod his head, slowly and thoughtfully. "Yes, of course," he agreed. "They're hunting you hard, and you're giving 'em a bully chase. But they'll get you, even up there. And I'm—sorry."

Their hands unclasped. Conniston filled his pipe and lighted it. Keith noticed that he held the lighted taper without a tremor. The nerve of the man was magnificent.

"I'm sorry," he said again. "I—like you. Do you know, Keith, I wish we'd been born brothers and you hadn't killed a man. That night I slipped the ring-dogs on you I felt almost like a devil. I wouldn't say it if it wasn't for this bally lung. But what's the use of keeping it back now? It doesn't seem fair to keep a man up in that place for three years, running from hole to hole like a rat, and then take him down for a hanging. I know it isn't fair in your case. I feel it. I don't mean to be inquisitive, old chap, but I'm not believing Departmental 'facts' any more. I'd make a topping good wager you're not the sort they make you out. And so I'd like to know—just why—you killed Judge Kirkstone?"

Keith's two fists knotted in the center of the table. Conniston saw his blue eyes darken for an instant with a savage fire. In that moment there

7

came a strange silence over the cabin, and in that silence the incessant and maddening yapping of the little white foxes rose shrilly over the distant booming and rumbling of the ice.

CHAPTER 2

"Why did I kill Judge Kirkstone?" Keith repeated the words slowly.

His clenched hands relaxed, but his eyes held the steady glow of fire. "What do the Departmental 'facts' tell you, Conniston?"

"That you murdered him in cold blood, and that the honor of the Service is at stake until you are hung."

"There's a lot in the view-point, isn't there? What if I said I didn't kill Judge Kirkstone?"

Conniston leaned forward a little too eagerly. The deadly paroxysm shook his frame again, and when it was over his breath came pantingly, as if hissing through a sieve. "My God, not Sunday—or Saturday," he breathed. "Keith, it's coming TOMORROW!"

"No, no, not then," said Keith, choking back something that rose in his throat. "You'd better lie down again."

Conniston gathered new strength. "And die like a rabbit? No, thank you, old chap! I'm after facts, and you can't lie to a dying man. Did you kill Judge Kirkstone?"

"I—don't—know," replied Keith slowly, looking steadily into the other's eyes. "I think so, and yet I am not positive. I went to his home that night with the determination to wring justice from him or kill him. I wish you could look at it all with my eyes, Conniston. You could if you had known my father. You see, my mother died when I was a little chap, and my father and I grew up together, chums. I don't believe I ever thought of him as just simply a father. Fathers are common. He was more than that. From the time I was ten years old we were inseparable. I guess I was twenty before he told me of the deadly feud that existed between him and Kirkstone, and it never troubled me much—because I didn't think anything would ever come of it—until Kirkstone got him. Then I realized that all through the years the old rattlesnake had been watching for his chance. It was a frame-up from beginning to end, and my father stepped into the trap. Even then he thought that his political enemies, and not Kirkstone, were at the bottom of it. We soon discovered the truth. My father got ten years. He was innocent. And the only man on earth who could prove his innocence was Kirkstone, the man who was gloating like a Shylock over his pound of flesh. Conniston, if you had known these things and had been in my shoes, what would you have done?"

9

Conniston, lighting another taper over the oil flame, hesitated and answered: "I don't know yet, old chap. What did you do?"

"I fairly got down on my knees to the scoundrel," resumed Keith. "If ever a man begged for another man's life, I begged for my father's—for the few words from Kirkstone that would set him free. I offered everything I had in the world, even my body and soul. God, I'll never forget that night! He sat there, fat and oily, two big rings on his stubby fingers—a monstrous toad in human form—and he chuckled and laughed at me in his joy, as though I were a mountebank playing amusing tricks for him—and there my soul was bleeding itself out before his eyes! And his son came in, fat and oily and accursed like his father, and HE laughed at me. I didn't know that such hatred could exist in the world, or that vengeance could bring such hellish joy. I could still hear their gloating laughter when I stumbled out into the night. It haunted me. I heard it in the trees. It came in the wind. My brain was filled with it—and suddenly I turned back, and I went into that house again without knocking, and I faced the two of them alone once more in that room. And this time, Conniston, I went back to get justice—or to kill. Thus far it was premeditated, but I went with my naked hands. There was a key in the door, and I locked it. Then I made my demand. I wasted no words—"

Keith rose from the table and began to pace back and forth. The wind had died again. They could hear the yapping of the foxes and the low thunder of the ice.

"The son began it," said Keith. "He sprang at me. I struck him. We grappled, and then the beast himself leaped at me with some sort of weapon in his hand. I couldn't see what it was, but it was heavy. The first blow almost broke my shoulder. In the scuffle I wrenched it from his hand, and then I found it was a long, rectangular bar of copper made for a paperweight. In that same instant I saw the son snatch up a similar object from the table, and in the act he smashed the table light. In darkness we fought. I did not feel that I was fighting men. They were monsters and gave me the horrible sensation of being in darkness with crawling serpents. Yes, I struck hard. And the son was striking, and neither of us could see. I felt my weapon hit, and it was then that Kirkstone crumpled down with a blubbery wheeze. You know what happened after that. The next morning only one copper weight was found in that room. The son had done away with the other. And the one that was left was covered with Kirkstone's blood and hair. There was no chance for me. So I got away. Six months later my father died in prison, and for three years I've been hunted as a fox is hunted

10

by the hounds. That's all, Conniston. Did I kill Judge Kirkstone? And, if I killed him, do you think I'm sorry for it, even though I hang?"

"Sit down!"

The Englishman's voice was commanding. Keith dropped back to his seat, breathing hard. He saw a strange light in the steely blue eyes of Conniston.

"Keith, when a man knows he's going to live, he is blind to a lot of things. But when he knows he's going to die, it's different. If you had told me that story a month ago, I'd have taken you down to the hangman just the same. It would have been my duty, you know, and I might have argued you were lying. But you can't lie to me—now. Kirkstone deserved to die. And so I've made up my mind what you're going to do. You're not going back to Coronation Gulf. You're going south. You're going back into God's country again. And you're not going as John Keith, the murderer, but as Derwent Conniston of His Majesty's Royal Northwest Mounted Police! Do you get me, Keith? Do you understand?"

Keith simply stared. The Englishman twisted a mustache, a half-humorous gleam in his eyes. He had been thinking of this plan of his for some time, and he had foreseen just how it would take Keith off his feet.

"Quite a scheme, don't you think, old chap? I like you. I don't mind saying I think a lot of you, and there isn't any reason on earth why you shouldn't go on living in my shoes. There's no moral objection. No one will miss me. I was the black sheep back in England—younger brother and all that—and when I had to choose between Africa and Canada, I chose Canada. An Englishman's pride is the biggest fool thing on earth, Keith, and I suppose all of them over there think I'm dead. They haven't heard from me in six or seven years. I'm forgotten. And the beautiful thing about this scheme is that we look so deucedly alike, you know. Trim that mustache and beard of yours a little, add a bit of a scar over your right eye, and you can walk in on old McDowell himself, and I'll wager he'll jump up and say, 'Bless my heart, if it isn't Conniston!' That's all I've got to leave you, Keith, a dead man's clothes and name. But you're welcome. They'll be of no more use to me after tomorrow."

"Impossible!" gasped Keith. "Conniston, do you know what you are saying?"

"Positively, old chap. I count every word, because it hurts when I talk. So you won't argue with me, please. It's the biggest sporting thing that's ever come my way. I'll be dead. You can bury me under this floor, where the foxes can't get at me. But my name will go on living and you'll wear my clothes back to civilization and tell McDowell how you got your man and how he died up here with a frosted lung. As proof of it you'll lug your own clothes down in a bundle along with any other little identifying things you may have, and there's a sergeancy waiting. McDowell promised it to you— if you got your man. Understand? And McDowell hasn't seen me for two years and three months, so if I MIGHT look a bit different to him, it would be natural, for you and I have been on the rough edge of the world all that time. The jolly good part of it all is that we look so much alike. I say the idea is splendid!"

Conniston rose above the presence of death in the thrill of the great gamble he was projecting. And Keith, whose heart was pounding like an excited fist, saw in a flash the amazing audacity of the thing that was in Conniston's mind, and felt the responsive thrill of its possibilities. No one down there would recognize in him the John Keith of four years ago. Then he was smooth-faced, with shoulders that stooped a little and a body that was not too strong. Now he was an animal! A four years' fight with the raw things of life had made him that, and inch for inch he measured up with Conniston. And Conniston, sitting opposite him, looked enough like him to be a twin brother. He seemed to read the thought in Keith's mind. There was an amused glitter in his eyes.

"I suppose it's largely because of the hair on our faces," he said. "You know a beard can cover a multitude of physical sins—and differences, old chap. I wore mine two years before I started out after you, vandyked rather carefully, you understand, so you'd better not use a razor. Physically you won't run a ghost of a chance of being caught. You'll look the part. The real fun is coming in other ways. In the next twenty-four hours you've got to learn by heart the history of Derwent Conniston from the day he joined the Royal Mounted. We won't go back further than that, for it wouldn't interest you, and ancient history won't turn up to trouble you. Your biggest danger will be with McDowell, commanding F Division at Prince Albert. He's a human fox of the old military school, mustaches and all, and he can see through boiler-plate. But he's got a big heart. He has been a good friend of mine, so along with Derwent Conniston's story you've got to load up with a lot about McDowell, too. There are many things—OH, GOD—"

He flung a hand to his chest. Grim horror settled in the little cabin as the cough convulsed him. And over it the wind shrieked again, swallowing up the yapping of the foxes and the rumble of the ice.

That night, in the yellow sputter of the seal-oil lamp, the fight began. Grim-faced—one realizing the nearness of death and struggling to hold it

12

back, the other praying for time—two men went through the amazing process of trading their identities. From the beginning it was Conniston's fight. And Keith, looking at him, knew that in this last mighty effort to die game the Englishman was narrowing the slight margin of hours ahead of him. Keith had loved but one man, his father. In this fight he learned to love another, Conniston. And once he cried out bitterly that it was unfair, that Conniston should live and he should die. The dying Englishman smiled and laid a hand on his, and Keith felt that the hand was damp with a cold sweat.

Through the terrible hours that followed Keith felt the strength and courage of the dying man becoming slowly a part of himself. The thing was epic. Conniston, throttling his own agony, was magnificent. And Keith felt his warped and despairing soul swelling with a new life and a new hope, and he was thrilled by the thought of what he must do to live up to the mark of the Englishman. Conniston's story was of the important things first. It began with his acquaintance with McDowell. And then, between the paroxysms that stained his lips red, he filled in with incident and smiled wanly as he told how McDowell had sworn him to secrecy once in the matter of an incident which the chief did not want the barracks to know—and laugh over. A very sensitive man in some ways was McDowell! At the end of the first hour Keith stood up in the middle of the floor, and with his arms resting on the table and his shoulders sagging Conniston put him through the drill. After that he gave Keith his worn Service Manual and commanded him to study while he rested. Keith helped him to his bunk, and for a time after that tried to read the Service book. But his eyes blurred, and his brain refused to obey. The agony in the Englishman's low breathing oppressed him with a physical pain. Keith felt himself choking and rose at last from the table and went out into the gray, ghostly twilight of the night.

His lungs drank in the ice-tanged air. But it was not cold. Kwaske-hoo—the change—had come. The air was filled with the tumult of the last fight of winter against the invasion of spring, and the forces of winter were crumbling. The earth under Keith's feet trembled in the mighty throes of their dissolution. He could hear more clearly the roar and snarl and rending thunder of the great fields of ice as they swept down with the arctic current into Hudson's Bay. Over him hovered a strange night. It was not black but a weird and wraith-like gray, and out of this sepulchral chaos came strange sounds and the moaning of a wind high up. A little while longer, Keith thought, and the thing would have driven him mad. Even now he fancied he heard the screaming and wailing of voices far up under the hidden stars. More than once in the past months he had listened to the sobbing of little

13

children, the agony of weeping women, and the taunting of wind voices that were either tormenting or crying out in a ghoulish triumph; and more than once in those months he had seen Eskimos—born in that hell but driven mad in the torture of its long night—rend the clothes from their bodies and plunge naked out into the pitiless gloom and cold to die. Conniston would never know how near the final breakdown his brain had been in that hour when he made him a prisoner. And Keith had not told him. The man-hunter had saved him from going mad. But Keith had kept that secret to himself.

Even now he shrank down as a blast of wind shot out of the chaos above and smote the cabin with a shriek that had in it a peculiarly penetrating note. And then he squared his shoulders and laughed, and the yapping of the foxes no longer filled him with a shuddering torment. Beyond them he was seeing home. God's country! Green forests and waters spattered with golden sun—things he had almost forgotten; once more the faces of women who were white. And with those faces he heard the voice of his people and the song of birds and felt under his feet the velvety touch of earth that was bathed in the aroma of flowers. Yes, he had almost forgotten those things. Yesterday they had been with him only as moldering skeletons—phantasmal dream-things—because he was going mad, but now they were real, they were just off there to the south, and he was going to them. He stretched up his arms, and a cry rose out of his throat. It was of triumph, of final exaltation. Three years of THAT—and he had lived through it! Three years of dodging from burrow to burrow, just as Conniston had said, like a hunted fox; three years of starvation, of freezing, of loneliness so great that his soul had broken—and now he was going home!

He turned again to the cabin, and when he entered the pale face of the dying Englishman greeted him from the dim glow of the yellow light at the table. And Conniston was smiling in a quizzical, distressed sort of way, with a hand at his chest. His open watch on the table pointed to the hour of midnight when the lesson went on.

Still later he heated the muzzle of his revolver in the flame of the seal-oil.

"It will hurt, old chap—putting this scar over your eye. But it's got to be done. I say, won't it be a ripping joke on McDowell?" Softly he repeated it, smiling into Keith's eyes. "A ripping joke—on McDowell!"

CHAPTER 3

Dawn—the dusk of another night—and Keith raised his haggard face from Conniston's bedside with a woman's sob on his lips. The Englishman had died as he knew that he would die, game to the last threadbare breath that came out of his body. For with this last breath he whispered the words which he had repeated a dozen times before, "Remember, old chap, you win or lose the moment McDowell first sets his eyes on you!" And then, with a strange kind of sob in his chest, he was gone, and Keith's eyes were blinded by the miracle of a hot flood of tears, and there rose in him a mighty pride in the name of Derwent Conniston.

It was his name now. John Keith was dead. It was Derwent Conniston who was living. And as he looked down into the cold, still face of the heroic Englishman, the thing did not seem so strange to him after all. It would not be difficult to bear Conniston's name; the difficulty would be in living up to the Conniston code.

That night the rumble of the ice fields was clearer because there was no wind to deaden their tumult. The sky was cloudless, and the stars were like glaring, yellow eyes peering through holes in a vast, overhanging curtain of jet black. Keith, out to fill his lungs with air, looked up at the phenomenon of the polar night and shuddered. The stars were like living things, and they were looking at him. Under their sinister glow the foxes were holding high carnival. It seemed to Keith that they had drawn a closer circle about the cabin and that there was a different note in their yapping now, a note that was more persistent, more horrible. Conniston had foreseen that closing-in of the little white beasts of the night, and Keith, reentering the cabin, set about the fulfillment of his promise. Ghostly dawn found his task completed.

Half an hour later he stood in the edge of the scrub timber that rimmed in the arctic plain, and looked for the last time upon the little cabin under the floor of which the Englishman was buried. It stood there splendidly unafraid in its terrible loneliness, a proud monument to a dead man's courage and a dead man's soul. Within its four walls it treasured a thing which gave to it at last a reason for being, a reason for fighting against dissolution as long as one log could hold upon another. Conniston's spirit had become a living part of it, and the foxes might yap everlastingly, and the winds howl, and winter follow winter, and long night follow long night—and it would stand there in its pride fighting to the last, a memorial to Derwent Conniston, the Englishman.

Looking back at it, Keith bared his head in the raw dawn. "God bless you, Conniston," he whispered, and turned slowly away and into the south.

Ahead of him was eight hundred miles of wilderness—eight hundred miles between him and the little town on the Saskatchewan where McDowell commanded Division of the Royal Mounted. The thought of distance did not appall him. Four years at the top of the earth had accustomed him to the illimitable and had inured him to the lack of things. That winter Conniston had followed him with the tenacity of a ferret for a thousand miles along the rim of the Arctic, and it had been a miracle that he had not killed the Englishman. A score of times he might have ended the exciting chase without staining his own hands. His Eskimo friends would have performed the deed at a word. But he had let the Englishman live, and Conniston, dead, was sending him back home. Eight hundred miles was but the step between.

He had no dogs or sledge. His own team had given up the ghost long ago, and a treacherous Kogmollock from the Roes Welcome had stolen the Englishman's outfit in the last lap of their race down from Fullerton's Point. What he carried was Conniston's, with the exception of his rifle and his own parka and hood. He even wore Conniston's watch. His pack was light. The chief articles it contained were a little flour, a three-pound tent, a sleeping-bag, and certain articles of identification to prove the death of John Keith, the outlaw. Hour after hour of that first day the zip, zip, zip of his snowshoes beat with deadly monotony upon his brain. He could not think. Time and again it seemed to him that something was pulling him back, and always he was hearing Conniston's voice and seeing Conniston's face in the gray gloom of the day about him. He passed through the slim finger of scrub timber that a strange freak of nature had flung across the plain, and once more was a moving speck in a wide and wind-swept barren. In the afternoon he made out a dark rim on the southern horizon and knew it was timber, real timber, the first he had seen since that day, a year and a half ago, when the last of the Mackenzie River forest had faded away behind him! It gave him, at last, something tangible to grip. It was a thing beckoning to him, a sentient, living wall beyond which was his other world. The eight hundred miles meant less to him than the space between himself and that growing, black rim on the horizon.

He reached it as the twilight of the day was dissolving into the deeper dusk of the night, and put up his tent in the shelter of a clump of gnarled and storm-beaten spruce. Then he gathered wood and built himself a fire. He did not count the sticks as he had counted them for eighteen months. He was wasteful, prodigal. He had traveled forty miles since morning but he felt no exhaustion. He gathered wood until he had a great pile of it, and the flames of his fire leaped higher and higher until the spruce needles crackled and hissed over his head. He boiled a pot of weak tea and made a supper of caribou meat and a bit of bannock. Then he sat with his back to a tree and stared into the flames.

The fire leaping and crackling before his eyes was like a powerful medicine. It stirred things that had lain dormant within him. It consumed the heavy dross of four years of stupefying torture and brought back to him vividly the happenings of a yesterday that had dragged itself on like a century. All at once he seemed unburdened of shackles that had weighted him down to the point of madness. Every fiber in his body responded to that glorious roar of the fire; a thing seemed to snap in his head, freeing it of an oppressive bondage, and in the heart of the flames he saw home, and hope, and life—the things familiar and precious long ago, which the scourge of the north had almost beaten dead in his memory. He saw the broad Saskatchewan shimmering its way through the yellow plains, banked in by the foothills and the golden mists of morning dawn; he saw his home town clinging to its shore on one side and with its back against the purple wilderness on the other; he heard the rhythmic chug, chug, chug of the old gold dredge and the rattle of its chains as it devoured its tons of sand for a few grains of treasure; over him there were lacy clouds in a blue heaven again, he heard the sound of voices, the tread of feet, laughter—life. His soul reborn, he rose to his feet and stretched his arms until the muscles snapped. No, they would not know him back there—now! He laughed softly as he thought of the old John Keith—"Johnny" they used to call him up and down the few balsam-scented streets—his father's right-hand man mentally but a little off feed, as his chum, Reddy McTabb, used to say, when it came to the matter of muscle and brawn. He could look back on things without excitement now. Even hatred had burned itself out, and he found himself wondering if old Judge Kirkstone's house looked the same on the top of the hill, and if Miriam Kirkstone had come back to live there after that terrible night when he had returned to avenge his father.

Four years! It was not so very long, though the years had seemed like a lifetime to him. There would not be many changes. Everything would be the same—everything—except—the old home. That home he and his father had planned, and they had overseen the building of it, a chateau of logs a

17

little distance from the town, with the Saskatchewan sweeping below it and the forest at its doors. Masterless, it must have seen changes in those four years. Fumbling in his pocket, his fingers touched Conniston's watch. He drew it out and let the firelight play on the open dial. It was ten o'clock. In the back of the premier half of the case Conniston had at some time or another pasted a picture. It must have been a long time ago, for the face was faded and indistinct. The eyes alone were undimmed, and in the flash of the fire they took on a living glow as they looked at Keith. It was the face of a young girl—a schoolgirl, Keith thought, of ten or twelve. Yet the eyes seemed older; they seemed pleading with someone, speaking a message that had come spontaneously out of the soul of the child. Keith closed the watch. Its tick, tick, tick rose louder to his ears. He dropped it in his pocket. He could still hear it.

A pitch-filled spruce knot exploded with the startling vividness of a star bomb, and with it came a dull sort of mental shock to Keith. He was sure that for an instant he had seen Conniston's face and that the Englishman's eyes were looking at him as the eyes had looked at him out of the face in the watch. The deception was so real that it sent him back a step, staring, and then, his eyes striving to catch the illusion again, there fell upon him a realization of the tremendous strain he had been under for many hours. It had been days since he had slept soundly. Yet he was not sleepy now; he scarcely felt fatigue. The instinct of self-preservation made him arrange his sleeping-bag on a carpet of spruce boughs in the tent and go to bed.

Even then, for a long time, he lay in the grip of a harrowing wakefulness. He closed his eyes, but it was impossible for him to hold them closed. The sounds of the night came to him with painful distinctness—the crackling of the fire, the serpent-like hiss of the flaming pitch, the whispering of the tree tops, and the steady tick, tick, tick of Conniston's watch. And out on the barren, through the rim of sheltering trees, the wind was beginning to moan its everlasting whimper and sob of loneliness. In spite of his clenched hands and his fighting determination to hold it off, Keith fancied that he heard again—riding strangely in that wind—the sound of Conniston's voice. And suddenly he asked himself: What did it mean? What was it that Conniston had forgotten? What was it that Conniston had been trying to tell him all that day, when he had felt the presence of him in the gloom of the Barrens? Was it that Conniston wanted him to come back?

He tried to rid himself of the depressing insistence of that thought. And yet he was certain that in the last half-hour before death entered the cabin the Englishman had wanted to tell him something and had crucified the

18

desire. There was the triumph of an iron courage in those last words, "Remember, old chap, you win or lose the moment McDowell first sets his eyes on you!"—but in the next instant, as death sent home its thrust, Keith had caught a glimpse of Conniston's naked soul, and in that final moment when speech was gone forever, he knew that Conniston was fighting to make his lips utter words which he had left unspoken until too late. And Keith, listening to the moaning of the wind and the crackling of the fire, found himself repeating over and over again, "What was it he wanted to say?"

In a lull in the wind Conniston's watch seemed to beat like a heart in its case, and swiftly its tick, tick, ticked to his ears an answer, "Come back, come back, come back!"

With a cry at his own pitiable weakness, Keith thrust the thing far under his sleeping-bag, and there its sound was smothered. At last sleep overcame him like a restless anesthesia.

With the break of another day he came out of his tent and stirred the fire. There were still bits of burning ember, and these he fanned into life and added to their flame fresh fuel. He could not easily forget last night's torture, but its significance was gone. He laughed at his own folly and wondered what Conniston himself would have thought of his nervousness. For the first time in years he thought of the old days down at college where, among other things, he had made a mark for himself in psychology. He had considered himself an expert in the discussion and understanding of phenomena of the mind. Afterward he had lived up to the mark and had profited by his beliefs, and the fact that a simple relaxation of his mental machinery had so disturbed him last night amused him now. The solution was easy. It was his mind struggling to equilibrium after four years of brain-fag. And he felt better. His brain was clearer. He listened to the watch and found its ticking natural. He braced himself to another effort and whistled as he prepared his breakfast.

After that he packed his dunnage and continued south. He wondered if Conniston ever knew his Manual as he learned it now. At the end of the sixth day he could repeat it from cover to cover. Every hour he made it a practice to stop short and salute the trees about him. McDowell would not catch him there.

"I am Derwent Conniston," he kept telling himself. "John Keith is dead—dead. I buried him back there under the cabin, the cabin built by Sergeant Trossy and his patrol in nineteen hundred and eight. My name is Conniston—Derwent Conniston."

19

In his years of aloneness he had grown into the habit of talking to himself—or with himself—to keep up his courage and sanity. "Keith, old boy, we've got to fight it out," he would say. Now it was, "Conniston, old chap, we'll win or die." After the third day, he never spoke of John Keith except as a man who was dead. And over the dead John Keith he spread Conniston's mantle. "John Keith died game, sir," he said to McDowell, who was a tree. "He was the finest chap I ever knew."

On this sixth day came the miracle. For the first time in many months John Keith saw the sun. He had seen the murky glow of it before this, fighting to break through the pall of fog and haze that hung over the Barrens, but this sixth day it was the sun, the real sun, bursting in all its glory for a short space over the northern world. Each day after this the sun was nearer and warmer, as the arctic vapor clouds and frost smoke were left farther behind, and not until he had passed beyond the ice fogs entirely did Keith swing westward. He did not hurry, for now that he was out of his prison, he wanted time in which to feel the first exhilarating thrill of his freedom. And more than all else he knew that he must measure and test himself for the tremendous fight ahead of him.

Now that the sun and the blue sky had cleared his brain, he saw the hundred pit-falls in his way, the hundred little slips that might be made, the hundred traps waiting for any chance blunder on his part. Deliberately he was on his way to the hangman. Down there—every day of his life—he would rub elbows with him as he passed his fellow men in the street. He would never completely feel himself out of the presence of death. Day and night he must watch himself and guard himself, his tongue, his feet, his thoughts, never knowing in what hour the eyes of the law would pierce the veneer of his disguise and deliver his life as the forfeit. There were times when the contemplation of these things appalled him, and his mind turned to other channels of escape. And then—always—he heard Conniston's cool, fighting voice, and the red blood fired up in his veins, and he faced home.

He was Derwent Conniston. And never for an hour could he put out of his mind the one great mystifying question in this adventure of life and death, who was Derwent Conniston? Shred by shred he pieced together what little he knew, and always he arrived at the same futile end. An Englishman, dead to his family if he had one, an outcast or an expatriate— and the finest, bravest gentleman he had ever known. It was the WHYFORE of these things that stirred within him an emotion which he had never experienced before. The Englishman had grimly and determinedly taken his secret to the grave with him. To him, John Keith—who was now

20

Derwent Conniston—he had left an heritage of deep mystery and the mission, if he so chose, of discovering who he was, whence he had come— and why. Often he looked at the young girl's picture in the watch, and always he saw in her eyes something which made him think of Conniston as he lay in the last hour of his life. Undoubtedly the girl had grown into a woman now.

Days grew into weeks, and under Keith's feet the wet, sweet-smelling earth rose up through the last of the slush snow. Three hundred miles below the Barrens, he was in the Reindeer Lake country early in May. For a week he rested at a trapper's cabin on the Burntwood, and after that set out for Cumberland House. Ten days later he arrived at the post, and in the sunlit glow of the second evening afterward he built his camp-fire on the shore of the yellow Saskatchewan.

The mighty river, beloved from the days of his boyhood, sang to him again, that night, the wonderful things that time and grief had dimmed in his heart. The moon rose over it, a warm wind drifted out of the south, and Keith, smoking his pipe, sat for a long time listening to the soft murmur of it as it rolled past at his feet. For him it had always been more than the river. He had grown up with it, and it had become a part of him; it had mothered his earliest dreams and ambitions; on it he had sought his first adventures; it had been his chum, his friend, and his comrade, and the fancy struck him that in the murmuring voice of it tonight there was a gladness, a welcome, an exultation in his return. He looked out on its silvery bars shimmering in the moonlight, and a flood of memories swept upon him. Thirty years was not so long ago that he could not remember the beautiful mother who had told him stories as the sun went down and bedtime drew near. And vividly there stood out the wonderful tales of Kistachiwun, the river; how it was born away over in the mystery of the western mountains, away from the eyes and feet of men; how it came down from the mountains into the hills, and through the hills into the plains, broadening and deepening and growing mightier with every mile, until at last it swept past their door, bearing with it the golden grains of sand that made men rich. His father had pointed out the deep-beaten trails of buffalo to him and had told him stories of the Indians and of the land before white men came, so that between father and mother the river became his book of fables, his wonderland, the never-ending source of his treasured tales of childhood. And tonight the river was the one thing left to him. It was the one friend he could claim again, the one comrade he could open his arms to without fear of betrayal. And with the grief for things that once had lived and were now

21

dead, there came over him a strange sort of happiness, the spirit of the great river itself giving him consolation.

Stretching out his arms, he cried: "My old river—it's me—Johnny Keith! I've come back!"

And the river, whispering, seemed to answer him: "It's Johnny Keith! And he's come back! He's come back!"

CHAPTER 4

For a week John Keith followed up the shores of the Saskatchewan. It was a hundred and forty miles from the Hudson's Bay Company's post of Cumberland House to Prince Albert as the crow would fly, but Keith did not travel a homing line. Only now and then did he take advantage of a portage trail. Clinging to the river, his journey was lengthened by some sixty miles. Now that the hour for which Conniston had prepared him was so close at hand, he felt the need of this mighty, tongueless friend that had played such an intimate part in his life. It gave to him both courage and confidence, and in its company he could think more clearly. Nights he camped on its golden-yellow bars with the open stars over his head when he slept; his ears drank in the familiar sounds of long ago, for which he had yearned to the point of madness in his exile—the soft cries of the birds that hunted and mated in the glow of the moon, the friendly twit, twit, twit of the low-flying sand-pipers, the hoot of the owls, and the splash and sleepy voice of wildfowl already on their way up from the south. Out of that south, where in places the plains swept the forest back almost to the river's edge, he heard now and then the doglike barking of his little yellow friends of many an exciting horseback chase, the coyotes, and on the wilderness side, deep in the forest, the sinister howling of wolves. He was traveling, literally, the narrow pathway between two worlds. The river was that pathway. On the one hand, not so very far away, were the rolling prairies, green fields of grain, settlements and towns and the homes of men; on the other the wilderness lay to the water's edge with its doors still open to him. The seventh day a new sound came to his ears at dawn. It was the whistle of a train at Prince Albert.

There was no change in that whistle, and every nerve-string in his body responded to it with crying thrill. It was the first voice to greet his home-coming, and the sound of it rolled the yesterdays back upon him in a deluge. He knew where he was now; he recalled exactly what he would find at the next turn in the river. A few minutes later he heard the wheezy chug, chug, chug of the old gold dredge at McCoffin's Bend. It would be the Betty M., of course, with old Andy Duggan at the windlass, his black pipe in mouth, still scooping up the shifting sands as he had scooped them up for more than twenty years. He could see Andy sitting at his post, clouded in a halo of tobacco smoke, a red-bearded, shaggy-headed giant of a man whom the town affectionately called the River Pirate. All his life Andy had spent in digging gold out of the mountains or the river, and like grim death he had hung to the bars above and below McCoffin's Bend. Keith smiled as he remembered old Andy's passion for bacon. One could always find the perfume of bacon about the Betty M., and when Duggan went to town, there were those who swore they could smell it in his whiskers.

Keith left the river trail now for the old logging road. In spite of his long fight to steel himself for what Conniston had called the "psychological moment," he felt himself in the grip of an uncomfortable mental excitement. At last he was face to face with the great gamble. In a few hours he would play his one card. If he won, there was life ahead of him again, if he lost—death. The old question which he had struggled to down surged upon him. Was it worth the chance? Was it in an hour of madness that he and Conniston had pledged themselves to this amazing adventure? The forest was still with him. He could turn back. The game had not yet gone so far that he could not withdraw his hand—and for a space a powerful impulse moved him. And then, coming suddenly to the edge of the clearing at McCoffin's Bend, he saw the dredge close inshore, and striding up from the beach Andy Duggan himself! In another moment Keith had stepped forth and was holding up a hand in greeting.

He felt his heart thumping in an unfamiliar way as Duggan came on. Was it conceivable that the riverman would not recognize him? He forgot his beard, forgot the great change that four years had wrought in him. He remembered only that Duggan had been his friend, that a hundred times they had sat together in the quiet glow of long evenings, telling tales of the great river they both loved. And always Duggan's stories had been of that mystic paradise hidden away in the western mountains—the river's end, the paradise of golden lure, where the Saskatchewan was born amid towering peaks, and where Duggan—a long time ago—had quested for the treasure which he knew was hidden somewhere there. Four years had not changed Duggan. If anything his beard was redder and thicker and his hair shaggier than when Keith had last seen him. And then, following him from the Betsy M., Keith caught the everlasting scent of bacon. He devoured it in deep breaths. His soul cried out for it. Once he had grown tired of Duggan's bacon, but now he felt that he could go on eating it forever. As Duggan advanced, he was moved by a tremendous desire to stretch out his hand and say: "I'm John Keith. Don't you know me, Duggan?" Instead, he choked back his desire and said, "Fine morning!"

Duggan nodded uncertainly. He was evidently puzzled at not being able to place his man. "It's always fine on the river, rain 'r shine. Anybody who says it ain't is a God A'mighty liar!"

He was still the old Duggan, ready to fight for his river at the drop of a hat! Keith wanted to hug him. He shifted his pack and said:

"I've slept with it for a week—just to have it for company—on the way down from Cumberland House. Seems good to get back!" He took off his hat and met the riverman's eyes squarely. "Do you happen to know if McDowell is at barracks?" he asked.

"He is," said Duggan.

That was all. He was looking at Keith with a curious directness. Keith held his breath. He would have given a good deal to have seen behind Duggan's beard. There was a hard note in the riverman's voice, too. It puzzled him. And there was a flash of sullen fire in his eyes at the mention of McDowell's name. "The Inspector's there—sittin' tight," he added, and to Keith's amazement brushed past him without another word and disappeared into the bush.

This, at least, was not like the good-humored Duggan of four years ago. Keith replaced his hat and went on. At the farther side of the clearing he turned and looked back. Duggan stood in the open roadway, his hands thrust deep in his pockets, staring after him. Keith waved his hand, but Duggan did not respond. He stood like a sphinx, his big red beard glowing in the early sun, and watched Keith until he was gone.

To Keith this first experiment in the matter of testing an identity was a disappointment. It was not only disappointing but filled him with apprehension. It was true that Duggan had not recognized him as John Keith, BUT NEITHER HAD HE RECOGNIZED HIM AS DERWENT CONNISTON! And Duggan was not a man to forget in three or four years—or half a lifetime, for that matter. He saw himself facing a new and unexpected situation. What if McDowell, like Duggan, saw in him nothing more than a stranger? The Englishman's last words pounded in his head again like little fists beating home a truth, "You win or lose the moment McDowell first sets his eyes on you." They pressed upon him now with a deadly significance. For the first time he understood all that Conniston had meant. His danger was not alone in the possibility of being recognized as John Keith; it lay also in the hazard of NOT being recognized as Derwent Conniston.

If the thought had come to him to turn back, if the voice of fear and a premonition of impending evil had urged him to seek freedom in another direction, their whispered cautions were futile in the thrill of the greater excitement that possessed him now. That there was a third hand playing in this game of chance in which Conniston had already lost his life, and in which he was now staking his own, was something which gave to Keith a new and entirely unlooked-for desire to see the end of the adventure. The mental vision of his own certain fate, should he lose, dissolved into a nebulous presence that no longer oppressed nor appalled him. Physical instinct to fight against odds, the inspiration that presages the uncertainty of battle, fired his blood with an exhilarating eagerness. He was anxious to stand face to face with McDowell. Not until then would the real fight begin. For the first time the fact seized upon him that the Englishman was wrong—he would NOT win or lose in the first moment of the Inspector's scrutiny. In that moment he could lose—McDowell's cleverly trained eyes might detect the fraud; but to win, if the game was not lost at the first shot, meant an exciting struggle. Today might be his Armageddon, but it could not possess the hour of his final triumph.

He felt himself now like a warrior held in leash within sound of the enemy's guns and the smell of his powder. He held his old world to be his enemy, for civilization meant people, and the people were the law—and the law wanted his life. Never had he possessed a deeper hatred for the old code of an eye for an eye and a tooth for a tooth than in this hour when he saw up the valley a gray mist of smoke rising over the roofs of his home town. He had never conceded within himself that he was a criminal. He believed that in killing Kirkstone he had killed a serpent who had deserved to die, and a hundred times he had told himself that the job would have been much more satisfactory from the view-point of human sanitation if he had sent the son in the father's footsteps. He had rid the people of a man not fit to live—and the people wanted to kill him for it. Therefore the men and women in that town he had once loved, and still loved, were his enemies, and to find friends among them again he was compelled to perpetrate a clever fraud.

He remembered an unboarded path from this side of the town, which entered an inconspicuous little street at the end of which was a barber shop. It was the barber shop which he must reach first He was glad that it was early in the day when he came to the street an hour later, for he would meet few people. The street had changed considerably. Long, open spaces had filled in with houses, and he wondered if the anticipated boom of four years ago had come. He smiled grimly as the humor of the situation struck him. His father and he had staked their future in accumulating a lot of "outside" property. If the boom had materialized, that property was "inside" now—and worth a great deal. Before he reached the barber shop he realized that the dream of the Prince Albertites had come true. Prosperity had advanced upon them in mighty leaps. The population of the place had trebled. He was a rich man! And also, it occurred to him, he was a dead one—or would be when he reported officially to McDowell. What a merry scrap there would be among the heirs of John Keith, deceased!

The old shop still clung to its corner, which was valuable as "business footage" now. But it possessed a new barber. He was alone. Keith gave his instructions in definite detail and showed him Conniston's photograph in his identification book. The beard and mustache must be just so, very smart, decidedly English, and of military neatness, his hair cut not too short and brushed smoothly back. When the operation was over, he congratulated the barber and himself. Bronzed to the color of an Indian by wind and smoke, straight as an arrow, his muscles swelling with the brute strength of the wilderness, he smiled at himself in the mirror when he compared the old John Keith with this new Derwent Conniston! Before he went out he tightened his belt a notch. Then he headed straight for the barracks of His Majesty's Royal Northwest Mounted Police.

His way took him up the main street, past the rows of shops that had been there four years ago, past the Saskatchewan Hotel and the little Board of Trade building which, like the old barber shop, still hung to its original perch at the edge of the high bank which ran precipitously down to the river. And there, as sure as fate, was Percival Clary, the little English Secretary! But what a different Percy!

He had broadened out and straightened up. He had grown a mustache, which was immaculately waxed. His trousers were immaculately creased, his shoes were shining, and he stood before the door of his now important office resting lightly on a cane. Keith grinned as he witnessed how prosperity had bolstered up Percival along with the town. His eyes quested for familiar faces as he went along. Here and there he saw one, but for the most part he encountered strangers, lively looking men who were hustling as if they had a mission in hand. Glaring real estate signs greeted him from every place of prominence, and automobiles began to hum up and down the main street that stretched along the river—twenty where there had been one not so long ago.

Keith found himself fighting to keep his eyes straight ahead when he met a girl or a woman. Never had he believed fully and utterly in the angelhood of the feminine until now. He passed perhaps a dozen on the way to barracks, and he was overwhelmed with the desire to stop and feast his eyes upon each one of them. He had never been a lover of women; he admired them, he believed them to be the better part of man, he had worshiped his mother, but his heart had been neither glorified nor broken by a passion for the opposite sex. Now, to the bottom of his soul, he worshiped that dozen! Some of them were homely, some of them were plain, two or three of them were pretty, but to Keith their present physical qualifications made no difference. They were white women, and they were glorious, every one of them! The plainest of them was lovely. He wanted to throw up his hat and shout in sheer joy. Four years—and now he was back in angel land! For a space he forgot McDowell.

His head was in a whirl when he came to barracks. Life was good, after all. It was worth fighting for, and he was bound fight. He went straight to McDowell's office. A moment after his knock on the door the Inspector's secretary appeared.

"The Inspector is busy, sir," he said in response to Keith's inquiry. "I'll tell him—"

"That I am here on a very important matter," advised Keith. "He will admit me when you tell him that I bring information regarding a certain John Keith."

The secretary disappeared through an inner door. It seemed not more than ten seconds before he was back. "The Inspector will see you, sir."

Keith drew a deep breath to quiet the violent beating of his heart. In spite of all his courage he felt upon him the clutch of a cold and foreboding hand, a hand that seemed struggling to drag him back. And again he heard Conniston's dying voice whispering to him, "REMEMBER, OLD CHAP, YOU WIN OR LOSE THE MOMENT MCDOWELL FIRST SETS HIS EYES ON YOU!"

Was Conniston right?

Win or lose, he would play the game as the Englishman would have played it. Squaring his shoulders he entered to face McDowell, the cleverest man-hunter in the Northwest.

CHAPTER 5

Keith's first vision, as he entered the office of the Inspector of Police, was not of McDowell, but of a girl. She sat directly facing him as he advanced through the door, the light from a window throwing into strong relief her face and hair. The effect was unusual. She was strikingly handsome. The sun, giving to the room a soft radiance, lit up her hair with shimmering gold; her eyes, Keith saw, were a clear and wonderful gray—and they stared at him as he entered, while the poise of her body and the tenseness of her face gave evidence of sudden and unusual emotion. These things Keith observed in a flash; then he turned toward McDowell.

The Inspector sat behind a table covered with maps and papers, and instantly Keith was conscious of the penetrating inquisition of his gaze. He felt, for an instant, the disquieting tremor of the criminal. Then he met McDowell's eyes squarely. They were, as Conniston had warned him, eyes that could see through boiler-plate. Of an indefinable color and deep set behind shaggy, gray eyebrows, they pierced him through at the first glance. Keith took in the carefully waxed gray mustaches, the close-cropped gray hair, the rigidly set muscles of the man's face, and saluted.

He felt creeping over him a slow chill. There was no greeting in that iron-like countenance, for full a quarter-minute no sign of recognition. And then, as the sun had played in the girl's hair, a new emotion passed over McDowell's face, and Keith saw for the first time the man whom Derwent Conniston had known as a friend as well as a superior. He rose from his chair, and leaning over the table said in a voice in which were mingled both amazement and pleasure:

"We were just talking about the devil—and here you are, sir! Conniston, how are you?"

For a few moments Keith did not see. HE HAD WON! The blood pounded through his heart so violently that it confused his vision and his senses. He felt the grip of McDowell's hand; he heard his voice; a vision swam before his eyes—and it was the vision of Derwent Conniston's triumphant face. He was standing erect, his head was up, he was meeting McDowell shoulder to shoulder, even smiling, but in that swift surge of exultation he did not know. McDowell, still gripping his hand and with his other hand on his arm, was wheeling him about, and he found the girl on her feet, staring at him as if he had newly risen from the dead.

McDowell's military voice was snapping vibrantly, "Conniston, meet Miss Miriam Kirkstone, daughter of Judge Kirkstone!"

He bowed and held for a moment in his own the hand of the girl whose father he had killed. It was lifeless and cold. Her lips moved, merely speaking his name. His own were mute. McDowell was saying something about the glory of the service and the sovereignty of the law. And then, breaking in like the beat of a drum on the introduction, his voice demanded, "Conniston—DID YOU GET YOUR MAN?"

The question brought Keith to his senses. He inclined his head slightly and said, "I beg to report that John Keith is dead, sir."

He saw Miriam Kirkstone give a visible start, as if his words had carried a stab. She was apparently making a strong effort to hide her agitation as she turned swiftly away from him, speaking to McDowell.

"You have been very kind, Inspector McDowell. I hope very soon to have the pleasure of talking with Mr. Conniston—about—John Keith."

She left them, nodding slightly to Keith.

When she was gone, a puzzled look filled the Inspector's eyes. "She has been like that for the last six months," he explained. "Tremendously interested in this man Keith and his fate. I don't believe that I have watched for your return more anxiously than she has, Conniston. And the curious part of it is she seemed to have no interest in the matter at all until six months ago. Sometimes I am afraid that brooding over her father's death has unsettled her a little. A mighty pretty girl, Conniston. A mighty pretty girl, indeed! And her brother is a skunk. Pst! You haven't forgotten him?"

He drew a chair up close to his own and motioned Keith to be seated. "You're changed, Conniston!"

The words came out of him like a shot. So unexpected were they that Keith felt the effect of them in every nerve of his body. He sensed instantly what McDowell meant. He was NOT like the Englishman; he lacked his mannerisms, his cool and superior suavity, the inimitable quality of his nerve and sportsmanship. Even as he met the disquieting directness of the Inspector's eyes, he could see Conniston sitting in his place, rolling his mustache between his forefinger and thumb, and smiling as though he had gone into the north but yesterday and had returned today. That was what McDowell was missing in him, the soul of Conniston himself—Conniston, the ne plus ultra of presence and amiable condescension, the man who could look the Inspector or the High Commissioner himself between the eyes, and, serenely indifferent to Service regulations, say, "Fine morning, old top!" Keith was not without his own sense of humor. How the

Englishman's ghost must be raging if it was in the room at the present moment! He grinned and shrugged his shoulders.

"Were you ever up there—through the Long Night—alone?" he asked. "Ever been through six months of living torture with the stars leering at you and the foxes barking at you all the time, fighting to keep yourself from going mad? I went through that twice to get John Keith, and I guess you're right. I'm changed. I don't think I'll ever be the same again. Something—has gone. I can't tell what it is, but I feel it. I guess only half of me pulled through. It killed John Keith. Rotten, isn't it?"

He felt that he had made a lucky stroke. McDowell pulled out a drawer from under the table and thrust a box of fat cigars under his nose.

"Light up, Derry—light up and tell us what happened. Bless my soul, you're not half dead! A week in the old town will straighten you out."

He struck a match and held it to the tip of Keith's cigar.

For an hour thereafter Keith told the story of the man-hunt. It was his Iliad. He could feel the presence of Conniston as words fell from his lips; he forgot the presence of the stern-faced man who was watching him and listening to him; he could see once more only the long months and years of that epic drama of one against one, of pursuit and flight, of hunger and cold, of the Long Nights filled with the desolation of madness and despair. He triumphed over himself, and it was Conniston who spoke from within him. It was the Englishman who told how terribly John Keith had been punished, and when he came to the final days in the lonely little cabin in the edge of the Barrens, Keith finished with a choking in his throat, and the words, "And that was how John Keith died—a gentleman and a MAN!"

He was thinking of the Englishman, of the calm and fearless smile in his eyes as he died, of his last words, the last friendly grip of his hand, and McDowell saw the thing as though he had faced it himself. He brushed a hand over his face as if to wipe away a film. For some moments after Keith had finished, he stood with his back to the man who he thought was Conniston, and his mind was swiftly adding twos and twos and fours and fours as he looked away into the green valley of the Saskatchewan. He was the iron man when he turned to Keith again, the law itself, merciless and potent, by some miracle turned into the form of human flesh.

"After two and a half years of THAT even a murderer must have seemed like a saint to you, Conniston. You have done your work splendidly. The whole story shall go to the Department, and if it doesn't bring you a commission, I'll resign. But we must continue to regret that John Keith did not live to be hanged."

"He has paid the price," said Keith dully.

"No, he has not paid the price, not in full. He merely died. It could have been paid only at the end of a rope. His crime was atrociously brutal, the culmination of a fiend's desire for revenge. We will wipe off his name. But I can not wipe away the regret. I would sacrifice a year of my life if he were in this room with you now. It would be worth it. God, what a thing for the Service—to have brought John Keith back to justice after four years!"

He was rubbing his hands and smiling at Keith even as he spoke. His eyes had taken on a filmy glitter. The law! It stood there, without heart or soul, coveting the life that had escaped it. A feeling of revulsion swept over Keith.

A knock came at the door.

McDowell's voice gave permission, and the door slowly opened. Cruze, the young secretary, thrust in his head.

"Shan Tung is waiting, sir," he said.

An invisible hand reached up suddenly and gripped at Keith's throat. He turned aside to conceal what his face might have betrayed. Shan Tung! He knew what it was now that had pulled him back, he knew why Conniston's troubled face had traveled with him over the Barrens, and there surged over him with a sickening foreboding, a realization of what it was that Conniston had remembered and wanted to tell him—when it was too late. THEY HAD FORGOTTEN SHAN TUNG, THE CHINAMAN!

CHAPTER 6

In the hall beyond the secretary's room Shan Tung waited. As McDowell was the iron and steel embodiment of the law, so Shan Tung was the flesh and blood spirit of the mysticism and immutability of his race. His face was the face of an image made of an unemotional living tissue in place of wood or stone, dispassionate, tolerant, patient. What passed in the brain behind his yellow-tinged eyes only Shan Tung knew. It was his secret. And McDowell had ceased to analyze or attempt to understand him. The law, baffled in its curiosity, had come to accept him as a weird and wonderful mechanism—a thing more than a man—possessed of an unholy power. This power was the oriental's marvelous ability to remember faces. Once Shan Tung looked at a face, it was photographed in his memory for years. Time and change could not make him forget—and the law made use of him.

Briefly McDowell had classified him at Headquarters. "Either an exiled prime minister of China or the devil in a yellow skin," he had written to the Commissioner. "Correct age unknown and past history a mystery. Dropped into Prince Albert in 1908 wearing diamonds and patent leather shoes. A stranger then and a stranger now. Proprietor and owner of the Shan Tung Cafe. Educated, soft-spoken, womanish, but the one man on earth I'd hate to be in a dark room with, knives drawn. I use him, mistrust him, watch him, and would fear him under certain conditions. As far as we can discover, he is harmless and law-abiding. But such a ferret must surely have played his game somewhere, at some time."

This was the man whom Conniston had forgotten and Keith now dreaded to meet. For many minutes Shan Tung had stood at a window looking out upon the sunlit drillground and the broad sweep of green beyond. He was toying with his slim hands caressingly. Half a smile was on his lips. No man had ever seen more than that half smile illuminate Shan Tung's face. His black hair was sleek and carefully trimmed. His dress was immaculate. His slimness, as McDowell had noted, was the slimness of a young girl.

When Cruze came to announce that McDowell would see him, Shan Tung was still visioning the golden-headed figure of Miriam Kirkstone as he had seen her passing through the sunshine. There was something like a purr in his breath as he stood interlacing his tapering fingers. The instant he heard the secretary's footsteps the finger play stopped, the purr died, the half smile was gone. He turned softly. Cruze did not speak. He simply made a movement of his head, and Shan Tung's feet fell noiselessly. Only the slight sound made by the opening and closing of a door gave evidence of his entrance into the Inspector's room. Shan Tung and no other could open and close a door like that. Cruze shivered. He always shivered when Shan Tung passed him, and always he swore that he could smell something in the air, like a poison left behind.

Keith, facing the window, was waiting. The moment the door was opened, he felt Shan Tung's presence. Every nerve in his body was keyed to an uncomfortable tension. The thought that his grip on himself was weakening, and because of a Chinaman, maddened him. And he must turn. Not to face Shan Tung now would be but a postponement of the ordeal and a confession of cowardice. Forcing his hand into Conniston's little trick of twisting a mustache, he turned slowly, leveling his eyes squarely to meet Shan Tung's.

To his surprise Shan Tung seemed utterly oblivious of his presence. He had not, apparently, taken more than a casual glance in his direction. In a voice which one beyond the door might have mistaken for a woman's, he was saying to McDowell:

"I have seen the man you sent me to see, Mr. McDowell. It is Larsen. He has changed much in eight years. He has grown a beard. He has lost an eye. His hair has whitened. But it is Larsen." The faultlessness of his speech and the unemotional but perfect inflection of his words made Keith, like the young secretary, shiver where he stood. In McDowell's face he saw a flash of exultation.

"He had no suspicion of you, Shan Tung?"

"He did not see me to suspect. He will be there—when—" Slowly he faced Keith. "—When Mr. Conniston goes to arrest him," he finished.

He inclined his head as he backed noiselessly toward the door. His yellow eyes did not leave Keith's face. In them Keith fancied that he caught a sinister gleam. There was the faintest inflection of a new note in his voice, and his fingers were playing again, but not as when he had looked out through the window at Miriam Kirkstone. And then—in a flash, it seemed to Keith—the Chinaman's eyes closed to narrow slits, and the pupils became points of flame no larger than the sharpened ends of a pair of pencils. The last that Keith was conscious of seeing of Shan Tung was the oriental's eyes. They had seemed to drag his soul half out of his body.

"A queer devil," said McDowell. "After he is gone, I always feel as if a snake had been in the room. He still hates you, Conniston. Three years have made no difference. He hates you like poison. I believe he would kill you, if he had a chance to do it and get away with the Business. And you—you blooming idiot—simply twiddle your mustache and laugh at him! I'd feel differently if I were in your boots."

Inwardly Keith was asking himself why it was that Shan Tung had hated Conniston.

McDowell added nothing to enlighten him. He was gathering up a number of papers scattered on his desk, smiling with a grim satisfaction. "It's Larsen all right if Shan Tung says so," he told Keith. And then, as if he had only thought of the matter, he said, "You're going to reenlist, aren't you, Conniston?"

"I still owe the Service a month or so before my term expires, don't I? After that—yes—I believe I shall reenlist."

"Good!" approved the Inspector. "I'll have you a sergeancy within a month. Meanwhile you're off duty and may do anything you please. You know Brady, the Company agent? He's up the Mackenzie on a trip, and here's the key to his shack. I know you'll appreciate getting under a real roof again, and Brady won't object as long as I collect his thirty dollars a month rent. Of course Barracks is open to you, but it just occurred to me you might prefer this place while on furlough. Everything is there from a bathtub to nutcrackers, and I know a little Jap in town who is hunting a job as a cook. What do you say?"

"Splendid!" cried Keith. "I'll go up at once, and if you'll hustle the Jap along, I'll appreciate it. You might tell him to bring up stuff for dinner," he added.

McDowell gave him a key. Ten minutes later he was out of sight of barracks and climbing a green slope that led to Brady's bungalow.

In spite of the fact that he had not played his part brilliantly, he believed that he had scored a triumph. Andy Duggan had not recognized him, and the riverman had been one of his most intimate friends. McDowell had accepted him apparently without a suspicion. And Shan Tung—

It was Shan Tung who weighed heavily upon his mind, even as his nerves tingled with the thrill of success. He could not get away from the vision of the Chinaman as he had backed through the Inspector's door, the flaming needle-points of his eyes piercing him as he went. It was not hatred he had seen in Shan Tung's face. He was sure of that. It was no emotion that he could describe. It was as if a pair of mechanical eyes fixed in the head of an amazingly efficient mechanical monster had focused themselves on him in those few instants. It made him think of an X-ray machine. But Shan Tung was human. And he was clever. Given another skin, one would not

35

have taken him for what he was. The immaculateness of his speech and manners was more than unusual; it was positively irritating, something which no Chinaman should rightfully possess. So argued Keith as he went up to Brady's bungalow.

He tried to throw off the oppression of the thing that was creeping over him, the growing suspicion that he had not passed safely under the battery of Shan Tung's eyes. With physical things he endeavored to thrust his mental uneasiness into the background. He lighted one of the half-dozen cigars McDowell had dropped into his pocket. It was good to feel a cigar between his teeth again and taste its flavor. At the crest of the slope on which Brady's bungalow stood, he stopped and looked about him. Instinctively his eyes turned first to the west. In that direction half of the town lay under him, and beyond its edge swept the timbered slopes, the river, and the green pathways of the plains. His heart beat a little faster as he looked. Half a mile away was a tiny, parklike patch of timber, and sheltered there, with the river running under it, was the old home. The building was hidden, but through a break in the trees he could see the top of the old red brick chimney glowing in the sun, as if beckoning a welcome to him over the tree tops. He forgot Shan Tung; he forgot McDowell; he forgot that he was John Keith, the murderer, in the overwhelming sea of loneliness that swept over him. He looked out into the world that had once been his, and all that he saw was that red brick chimney glowing in the sun, and the chimney changed until at last it seemed to him like a tombstone rising over the graves of the dead. He turned to the door of the bungalow with a thickening in his throat and his eyes filmed by a mist through which for a few moments it was difficult for him to see.

The bungalow was darkened by drawn curtains when he entered. One after another he let them up, and the sun poured in. Brady had left his place in order, and Keith felt about him an atmosphere of cheer that was a mighty urge to his flagging spirits. Brady was a home man without a wife. The Company's agent had called his place "The Shack" because it was built entirely of logs, and a woman could not have made it more comfortable. Keith stood in the big living-room. At one end was a strong fireplace in which kindlings and birch were already laid, waiting the touch of a match. Brady's reading table and his easy chair were drawn up close; his lounging moccasins were on a footstool; pipes, tobacco, books and magazines littered the table; and out of this cheering disorder rose triumphantly the amber shoulder of a half-filled bottle of Old Rye.

Keith found himself chuckling. His grin met the lifeless stare of a pair of glass eyes in the huge head of an old bull moose over the mantel, and after that his gaze rambled over the walls ornamented with mounted heads, pictures, snowshoes, gun-racks and the things which went to make up the comradeship and business of Brady's picturesque life. Keith could look through into the little dining-room, and beyond that was the kitchen. He made an inventory of both and found that McDowell was right. There were nutcrackers in Brady's establishment. And he found the bathroom. It was not much larger than a piano box, but the tub was man's size, and Keith raised a window and poked his head out to find that it was connected with a rainwater tank built by a genius, just high enough to give weight sufficient for a water system and low enough to gather the rain as it fell from the eaves. He laughed outright, the sort of laugh that comes out of a man's soul not when he is amused but when he is pleased. By the time he had investigated the two bedrooms, he felt a real affection for Brady. He selected the agent's room for his own. Here, too, were pipes and tobacco and books and magazines, and a reading lamp on a table close to the bedside. Not until he had made a closer inspection of the living-room did he discover that the Shack also had a telephone.

By that time he noted that the sun had gone out. Driving up from the west was a mass of storm clouds. He unlocked a door from which he could look up the river, and the wind that was riding softly in advance of the storm ruffled his hair and cooled his face. In it he caught again the old fancy—the smells of the vast reaches of unpeopled prairie beyond the rim of the forest, and the luring chill of the distant mountain tops. Always storm that came down with the river brought to him voice from the river's end. It came to him from the great mountains that were a passion with him; it seemed to thunder to him the old stories of the mightiest fastnesses of the Rockies and stirred in him the child-bred yearning to follow up his beloved river until he came at last to the mystery of its birthplace in the cradle of the western ranges. And now, as he faced the storm, the grip of that desire held him like a strong hand.

The sky blackened swiftly, and with the rumbling of far-away thunder he saw the lightning slitting the dark heaven like bayonets, and the fire of the electrical charges galloped to him and filled his veins. His heart all at once cried out words that his lips did not utter. Why should he not answer the call that had come to him through all the years? Now was the time—and why should he not go? Why tempt fate in the hazard of a great adventure where home and friends and even hope were dead to him, when off there beyond the storm was the place of his dreams? He threw out his arms. His voice broke at last in a cry of strange ecstasy. Not everything was gone! Not everything was dead! Over the graveyard of his past there was sweeping a mighty force that called him, something that was no longer merely an urge and a demand but a thing that was irresistible. He would go! Tomorrow—today—tonight—he would begin making plans!

He watched the deluge as it came on with a roar of wind, a beating, hissing wall under which the tree tops down in the edge of the plain bent their heads like a multitude of people in prayer. He saw it sweeping up the slope in a mass of gray dragoons. It caught him before he had closed the door, and his face dripped with wet as he forced the last inch of it against the wind with his shoulder. It was the sort of storm Keith liked. The thunder was the rumble of a million giant cartwheels rolling overhead.

Inside the bungalow it was growing dark as though evening had come. He dropped on his knees before the pile of dry fuel in the fireplace and struck a match. For a space the blaze smoldered; then the birch fired up like oil-soaked tinder, and a yellow flame crackled and roared up the flue. Keith was sensitive in the matter of smoking other people's pipes, so he drew out his own and filled it with Brady's tobacco. It was an English mixture, rich and aromatic, and as the fire burned brighter and the scent of the tobacco filled the room, he dropped into Brady's big lounging chair and stretched out his legs with a deep breath of satisfaction. His thoughts wandered to the clash of the storm. He would have a place like this out there in the mystery of the trackless mountains, where the Saskatchewan was born. He would build it like Brady's place, even to the rain-water tank midway between the roof and the ground. And after a few years no one would remember that a man named John Keith had ever lived.

Something brought him suddenly to his feet. It was the ringing of the telephone. After four years the sound was one that roused with an uncomfortable jump every nerve in his body. Probably it was McDowell calling up about the Jap or to ask how he liked the place. Probably—it was that. He repeated the thought aloud as he laid his pipe on the table. And yet as his hand came in contact with the telephone, he felt an inclination to draw back. A subtle voice whispered him not to answer, to leave while the storm was dark, to go back into the wilderness, to fight his way to the western mountains.

With a jerk he unhooked the receiver and put it to his ear.

It was not McDowell who answered him. It was not Shan Tung. To his amazement, coming to him through the tumult of the storm, he recognized the voice of Miriam Kirkstone!

CHAPTER 7

Why should Miriam Kirkstone call him up in an hour when the sky was livid with the flash of lightning and the earth trembled with the roll of thunder? This was the question that filled Keith's mind as he listened to the voice at the other end of the wire. It was pitched to a high treble as if unconsciously the speaker feared that the storm might break in upon her words. She was telling him that she had telephoned McDowell but had been too late to catch him before he left for Brady's bungalow; she was asking him to pardon her for intruding upon his time so soon after his return, but she was sure that he would understand her. She wanted him to come up to see her that evening at eight o'clock. It was important—to her. Would he come?

Before Keith had taken a moment to consult with himself he had replied that he would. He heard her "thank you," her "good-by," and hung up the receiver, stunned. So far as he could remember, he had spoken no more than seven words. The beautiful young woman up at the Kirkstone mansion had clearly betrayed her fear of the lightning by winding up her business with him at the earliest possible moment. Why, then, had she not waited until the storm was over?

A pounding at the door interrupted his thought. He went to it and admitted an individual who, in spite of his water-soaked condition, was smiling all over. It was Wallie, the Jap. He was no larger than a boy of sixteen, and from eyes, ears, nose, and hair he was dripping streams, while his coat bulged with packages which he had struggled to protect, from the torrent through which he had forced his way up the hill. Keith liked him on the instant. He found himself powerless to resist the infection of Wallie's grin, and as Wallie hustled into the kitchen like a wet spaniel, he followed and helped him unload. By the time the little Jap had disgorged his last package, he had assured Keith that the rain was nice, that his name was Wallie, that he expected five dollars a week and could cook "like heaven." Keith laughed outright, and Wallie was so delighted with the general outlook that he fairly kicked his heels together. Thereafter for an hour or so he was left alone in possession of the kitchen, and shortly Keith began to hear certain sounds and catch occasional odoriferous whiffs which assured him that Wallie was losing no time in demonstrating his divine efficiency in the matter of cooking.

Wallie's coming gave him an excuse to call up McDowell. He confessed to a disquieting desire to hear the inspector's voice again. In the back of his head was the fear of Shan Tung, and the hope that McDowell might throw some light on Miriam Kirkstone's unusual request to see her that night. The storm had settled down into a steady drizzle when he got in touch with him, and he was relieved to find there was no change in the friendliness of the voice that came over the telephone. If Shan Tung had a suspicion, he had kept it to himself.

To Keith's surprise it was McDowell who spoke first of Miss Kirkstone.

"She seemed unusually anxious to get in touch with you," he said. "I am frankly disturbed over a certain matter, Conniston, and I should like to talk with you before you go up tonight."

Keith sniffed the air. "Wallie is going to ring the dinner bell within half an hour. Why not slip on a raincoat and join me up here? I think it's going to be pretty good."

"I'll come," said McDowell. "Expect me any moment."

Fifteen minutes later Keith was helping him off with his wet slicker. He had expected McDowell to make some observation on the cheerfulness of the birch fire and the agreeable aromas that were leaking from Wallie's kitchen, but the inspector disappointed him. He stood for a few moments with his back to the fire, thumbing down the tobacco in his pipe, and he made no effort to conceal the fact that there was something in his mind more important than dinner and the cheer of a grate.

His eyes fell on the telephone, and he nodded toward it. "Seemed very anxious to see you, didn't she, Conniston? I mean Miss Kirkstone."

"Rather."

McDowell seated himself and lighted a match. "Seemed—a little—nervous—perhaps," he suggested between puffs. "As though something had happened—or was going to happen. Don't mind my questioning you, do you, Derry?"

"Not a bit," said Keith. "You see, I thought perhaps you might explain—"

There was a disquieting gleam in McDowell's eyes. "It was odd that she should call you up so soon—and in the storm—wasn't it? She expected to find you at my office. I could fairly hear the lightning hissing along the wires. She must have been under some unusual impulse."

"Perhaps."

McDowell was silent for a space, looking steadily at Keith, as if measuring him up to something.

"I don't mind telling you that I am very deeply interested in Miss Kirkstone," he said. "You didn't see her when the Judge was killed. She was away at school, and you were on John Keith's trail when she returned. I have never been much of a woman's man, Conniston, but I tell you frankly that up until six or eight months ago Miriam was one of the most beautiful girls I have ever seen. I would give a good deal to know the exact hour and date when the change in her began. I might be able to trace some event to that date. It was six months ago that she began to take an interest in the fate of John Keith. Since then the change in her has alarmed me, Conniston. I don't understand. She has betrayed nothing. But I have seen her dying by inches under my eyes. She is only a pale and drooping flower compared with what she was. I am positive it is not a sickness—unless it is mental. I have a suspicion. It is almost too terrible to put into words. You will be going up there tonight—you will be alone with her, will talk with her, may learn a great deal if you understand what it is that is eating like a canker in my mind. Will you help me to discover her secret?" He leaned toward Keith. He was no longer the man of iron. There was something intensely human in his face.

"There is no other man on earth I would confide this matter to," he went on slowly. "It will take—a gentleman—to handle it, someone who is big enough to forget if my suspicion is untrue, and who will understand fully what sacrilege means should it prove true. It is extremely delicate. I hesitate. And yet—I am waiting, Conniston. Is it necessary to ask you to pledge secrecy in the matter?"

Keith held out a hand. McDowell gripped it tight.

"It is—Shan Tung," he said, a peculiar hiss in his voice. "Shan Tung— and Miriam Kirkstone! Do you understand, Conniston? Does the horror of it get hold of you? Can you make yourself believe that it is possible? Am I mad to allow such a suspicion to creep into my brain? Shan Tung—Miriam Kirkstone! And she sees herself standing now at the very edge of the pit of hell, and it is killing her."

Keith felt his blood running cold as he saw in the inspector's face the thing which he did not put more plainly in word. He was shocked. He drew his hand from McDowell's grip almost fiercely.

"Impossible!" he cried. "Yes, you are mad. Such a thing would be inconceivable!"

"And yet I have told myself that it is possible," said McDowell. His face was returning into its iron-like mask. His two hands gripped the arms of his chair, and he stared at Keith again as if he were looking through him at something else, and to that something else he seemed to speak, slowly, weighing and measuring each word before it passed his lips. "I am not superstitious. It has always been a law with me to have conviction forced upon me. I do not believe unusual things until investigation proves them. I am making an exception in the case of Shan Tung. I have never regarded him as a man, like you and me, but as a sort of superphysical human machine possessed of a certain psychological power that is at times almost deadly. Do you begin to understand me? I believe that he has exerted the whole force of that influence upon Miriam Kirkstone—and she has surrendered to it. I believe—and yet I am not positive."

"And you have watched them for six months?"

"No. The suspicion came less than a month ago. No one that I know has ever had the opportunity of looking into Shan Tung's private life. The quarters behind his cafe are a mystery. I suppose they can be entered from the cafe and also from a little stairway at the rear. One night—very late—I saw Miriam Kirkstone come down that stairway. Twice in the last month she has visited Shan Tung at a late hour. Twice that I know of, you understand. And that is not all—quite."

Keith saw the distended veins in McDowell's clenched hands, and he knew that he was speaking under a tremendous strain.

"I watched the Kirkstone home—personally. Three times in that same month Shan Tung visited her there. The third time I entered boldly with a fraud message for the girl. I remained with her for an hour. In that time I saw nothing and heard nothing of Shan Tung. He was hiding—or got out as I came in."

Keith was visioning Miriam Kirkstone as he had seen her in the inspector's office. He recalled vividly the slim, golden beauty of her, the wonderful gray of her eyes, and the shimmer of her hair as she stood in the light of the window—and then he saw Shan Tung, effeminate, with his sly, creeping hands and his narrowed eyes, and the thing which McDowell had suggested rose up before him a monstrous impossibility.

"Why don't you demand an explanation of Miss Kirkstone?" he asked.

"I have, and she denies it all absolutely, except that Shan Tung came to her house once to see her brother. She says that she was never on the little stairway back of Shan Tung's place."

"And you do not believe her?"

"Assuredly not. I saw her. To speak the cold truth, Conniston, she is lying magnificently to cover up something which she does not want any other person on earth to know."

Keith leaned forward suddenly. "And why is it that John Keith, dead and buried, should have anything to do with this?" he demanded. "Why did this 'intense interest' you speak of in John Keith begin at about the same time your suspicions began to include Shan Tung?"

McDowell shook his head. "It may be that her interest was not so much in John Keith as in you, Conniston. That is for you to discover—tonight. It is an interesting situation. It has tragic possibilities. The instant you substantiate my suspicions we'll deal directly with Shan Tung. Just now— there's Wallie behind you grinning like a Cheshire cat. His dinner must be a success."

The diminutive Jap had noiselessly opened the door of the little dining-room in which the table was set for two.

Keith smiled as he sat down opposite the man who would have sent him to the executioner had he known the truth. After all, it was but a step from comedy to tragedy. And just now he was conscious of a bit of grisly humor in the situation.

CHAPTER 8

The storm had settled into a steady drizzle when McDowell left the Shack at two o'clock. Keith watched the iron man, as his tall, gray figure faded away into the mist down the slope, with a curious undercurrent of emotion. Before the inspector had come up as his guest he had, he thought, definitely decided his future action. He would go west on his furlough, write McDowell that he had decided not to reenlist, and bury himself in the British Columbia mountains before an answer could get back to him, leaving the impression that he was going on to Australia or Japan. He was not so sure of himself now. He found himself looking ahead to the night, when he would see Miriam Kirkstone, and he no longer feared Shan Tung as he had feared him a few hours before. McDowell himself had given him new weapons. He was unofficially on Shan Tung's trail. McDowell had frankly placed the affair of Miriam Kirkstone in his hands. That it all had in some mysterious way something to do with himself—John Keith—urged him on to the adventure.

He waited impatiently for the evening. Wallie, smothered in a great raincoat, he sent forth on a general foraging expedition and to bring up some of Conniston's clothes. It was a quarter of eight when he left for Miriam Kirkstone's home.

Even at that early hour the night lay about him heavy and dark and saturated with a heavy mist. From the summit of the hill he could no longer make out the valley of the Saskatchewan. He walked down into a pit in which the scattered lights of the town burned dully like distant stars. It was a little after eight when he came to the Kirkstone house. It was set well back in an iron-fenced area thick with trees and shrubbery, and he saw that the porch light was burning to show him the way. Curtains were drawn, but a glow of warm light lay behind them.

He was sure that Miriam Kirkstone must have heard the crunch of his feet on the gravel walk, for he had scarcely touched the old-fashioned knocker on the door when the door itself was opened. It was Miriam who greeted him. Again he held her hand for a moment in his own.

It was not cold, as it had been in McDowell's office. It was almost feverishly hot, and the pupils of the girl's eyes were big, and dark, and filled with a luminous fire. Keith might have thought that coming in out of the dark night he had startled her. But it was not that. She was repressing something that had preceded him. He thought that he heard the almost

45

noiseless closing of a door at the end of the long hall, and his nostrils caught the faint aroma of a strange perfume. Between him and the light hung a filmy veil of smoke. He knew that it had come from a cigarette. There was an uneasy note in Miss Kirkstone's voice as she invited him to hang his coat and hat on an old-fashioned rack near the door. He took his time, trying to recall where he had detected that perfume before. He remembered, with a sort of shock. It was after Shan Tung had left McDowell's office.

She was smiling when he turned, and apologizing again for making her unusual request that day.

"It was—quite unconventional. But I felt that you would understand, Mr. Conniston. I guess I didn't stop to think. And I am afraid of lightning, too. But I wanted to see you. I didn't want to wait until tomorrow to hear about what happened up there. Is it—so strange?"

Afterward he could not remember just what sort of answer he made. She turned, and he followed her through the big, square-cut door leading out of the hall. It was the same door with the great, sliding panel he had locked on that fateful night, years ago, when he had fought with her father and brother. In it, for a moment, her slim figure was profiled in a frame of vivid light. Her mother must have been beautiful. That was the thought that flashed upon him as the room and its tragic memory lay before him. Everything came back to him vividly, and he was astonished at the few changes in it. There was the big chair with its leather arms, in which the overfatted creature who had been her father was sitting when he came in. It was the same table, too, and it seemed to him that the same odds and ends were on the mantel over the cobblestone fireplace. And there was somebody's picture of the Madonna still hanging between two windows. The Madonna, like the master of the house, had been too fat to be beautiful. The son, an ogreish pattern of his father, had stood with his back to the Madonna, whose overfat arms had seemed to rest on his shoulders. He remembered that.

The girl was watching him closely when he turned toward her. He had frankly looked the room over, without concealing his intention. She was breathing a little unsteadily, and her hair was shimmering gloriously in the light of an overhead chandelier. She sat down with that light over her, motioning him to be seated opposite her—across the same table from which he had snatched the copper weight that had killed Kirkstone. He had never seen anything quite so steady, quite so beautiful as her eyes when they looked across at him. He thought of McDowell's suspicion and of Shan

46

Tung and gripped himself hard. The same strange perfume hung subtly on the air he was breathing. On a small silver tray at his elbow lay the ends of three freshly burned cigarettes.

"Of course you remember this room?"

He nodded. "Yes. It was night when I came, like this. The next day I went after John Keith."

She leaned toward him, her hands clasped in front of her on the table. "You will tell me the truth about John Keith?" she asked in a low, tense voice. "You swear that it will be the truth?"

"I will keep nothing back from you that I have told Inspector McDowell," he answered, fighting to meet her eyes steadily. "I almost believe I may tell you more."

"Then—did you speak the truth when you reported to Inspector McDowell? IS JOHN KEITH DEAD?" Could Shan Tung meet those wonderful eyes as he was meeting them now, he wondered? Could he face them and master them, as McDowell had hinted? To McDowell the lie had come easily to his tongue. It stuck in his throat now. Without giving him time to prepare himself the girl had shot straight for the bull's-eye, straight to the heart of the thing that meant life or death to him, and for a moment he found no answer. Clearly he was facing suspicion. She could not have driven the shaft intuitively. The unexpectedness of the thing astonished him and then thrilled him, and in the thrill of it he found himself more than ever master of himself.

"Would you like to hear how utterly John Keith is dead and how he died?" he asked.

"Yes. That is what I must know."

He noticed that her hands had closed. Her slender fingers were clenched tight.

"I hesitate, because I have almost promised to tell you even more than I told McDowell," he went on. "And that will not be pleasant for you to hear. He killed your father. There can be no sympathy in your heart for John Keith. It will not be pleasant for you to hear that I liked the man, and that I am sorry he is dead."

"Go on—please."

Her hands unclasped. Her fingers lay limp. Something faded slowly out of her face. It was as if she had hoped for something, and that hope was dying. Could it be possible that she had hoped he would say that John Keith was alive?

"Did you know this man?" he asked.

47

"This John Keith?"

She shook her head. "No. I was away at school for many years. I don't remember him."

"But he knew you—that is, he had seen you," said Keith. "He used to talk to me about you in those days when he was helpless and dying. He said that he was sorry for you, and that only because of you did he ever regret the justice he brought upon your father. You see I speak his words. He called it justice. He never weakened on that point. You have probably never heard his part of the story."

"No."

The one word forced itself from her lips. She was expecting him to go on, and waited, her eyes never for an instant leaving his face.

He did not repeat the story exactly as he had told it to McDowell. The facts were the same, but the living fire of his own sympathy and his own conviction were in them now. He told it purely from Keith's point of view, and Miriam Kirkstone's face grew whiter, and her hands grew tense again, as she listened for the first time to Keith's own version of the tragedy of the room in which they were sitting. And then he followed Keith up into that land of ice and snow and gibbering Eskimos, and from that moment he was no longer Keith but spoke with the lips of Conniston. He described the sunless weeks and months of madness until the girl's eyes seemed to catch fire, and when at last he came to the little cabin in which Conniston had died, he was again John Keith. He could not have talked about himself as he did about the Englishman. And when he came to the point where he buried Conniston under the floor, a dry, broken sob broke in upon him from across the table. But there were no tears in the girl's eyes. Tears, perhaps, would have hidden from him the desolation he saw there. But she did not give in. Her white throat twitched. She tried to draw her breath steadily. And then she said:

"And that—was John Keith!"

He bowed his head in confirmation of the lie, and, thinking of Conniston, he said:

"He was the finest gentleman I ever knew. And I am sorry he is dead."

"And I, too, am sorry."

She was reaching a hand across the table to him, slowly, hesitatingly. He stared at her.

"You mean that?"

"Yes, I am sorry."

He took her hand. For a moment her fingers tightened about his own. Then they relaxed and drew gently away from him. In that moment he saw a sudden change come into her face. She was looking beyond him, over his right shoulder. Her eyes widened, her pupils dilated under his gaze, and she held her breath. With the swift caution of the man-hunted he turned. The room was empty behind him. There was nothing but a window at his back. The rain was drizzling against it, and he noticed that the curtain was not drawn, as they were drawn at the other windows. Even as he looked, the girl went to it and pulled down the shade. He knew that she had seen something, something that had startled her for a moment, but he did not question her. Instead, as if he had noticed nothing, he asked if he might light a cigar.

"I see someone smokes," he excused himself, nodding at the cigarette butts.

He was watching her closely and would have recalled the words in the next breath. He had caught her. Her brother was out of town. And there was a distinctly unAmerican perfume in the smoke that someone had left in the room. He saw the bit of red creeping up her throat into her cheeks, and his conscience shamed him. It was difficult for him not to believe McDowell now. Shan Tung had been there. It was Shan Tung who had left the hall as he entered. Probably it was Shan Tung whose face she had seen at the window.

What she said amazed him. "Yes, it is a shocking habit of mine, Mr. Conniston. I learned to smoke in the East. Is it so very bad, do you think?"

He fairly shook himself. He wanted to say, "You beautiful little liar, I'd like to call your bluff right now, but I won't, because I'm sorry for you!" Instead, he nipped off the end of his cigar, and said:

"In England, you know, the ladies smoke a great deal. Personally I may be a little prejudiced. I don't know that it is sinful, especially when one uses such good judgment—in orientals." And then he was powerless to hold himself back. He smiled at her frankly, unafraid. "I don't believe you smoke," he added.

He rose to his feet, still smiling across at her, like a big brother waiting for her confidence. She was not alarmed at the directness with which he had guessed the truth. She was no longer embarrassed. She seemed for a moment to be looking through him and into him, a strange and yearning desire glowing dully in her eyes. He saw her throat twitching again, and he was filled with an infinite compassion for this daughter of the man he had killed. But he kept it within himself. He had gone far enough. It was for her to speak. At the door she gave him her hand again, bidding him good-night. She looked pathetically helpless, and he thought that someone ought to be there with the right to take her in his arms and comfort her.

"You will come again?" she whispered.

"Yes, I am coming again," he said. "Good-night."

He passed out into the drizzle. The door closed behind him, but not before there came to him once more that choking sob from the throat of Miriam Kirkstone.

CHAPTER 9

Keith's hand was on the butt of his revolver as he made his way through the black night. He could not see the gravel path under his feet but could only feel it. Something that was more than a guess made him feel that Shan Tung was not far away, and he wondered if it was a premonition, and what it meant. With the keen instinct of a hound he was scenting for a personal danger. He passed through the gate and began the downward slope toward town, and not until then did he begin adding things together and analyzing the situation as it had transformed itself since he had stood in the door of the Shack, welcoming the storm from the western mountains. He thought that he had definitely made up his mind then; now it was chaotic. He could not leave Prince Albert immediately, as the inspiration had moved him a few hours before. McDowell had practically given him an assignment. And Miss Kirkstone was holding him. Also Shan Tung. He felt within himself the sensation of one who was traveling on very thin ice, yet he could not tell just where or why it was thin.

"Just a fool hunch," he assured himself.

"Why the deuce should I let a confounded Chinaman and a pretty girl get on my nerves at this stage of the game? If it wasn't for McDowell—"

And there he stopped. He had fought too long at the raw edge of things to allow himself to be persuaded by delusions, and he confessed that it was John Keith who was holding him, that in some inexplicable way John Keith, though officially dead and buried, was mixed up in a mysterious affair in which Miriam Kirkstone and Shan Tung were the moving factors. And inasmuch as he was now Derwent Conniston and no longer John Keith, he took the logical point of arguing that the affair was none of his business, and that he could go on to the mountains if he pleased. Only in that direction could he see ice of a sane and perfect thickness, to carry out the metaphor in his head. He could report indifferently to McDowell, forget Miss Kirkstone, and disappear from the menace of Shan Tung's eyes. John Keith, he repeated, would be officially dead, and being dead, the law would have no further interest in him.

He prodded himself on with this thought as he fumbled his way through darkness down into town. Miriam Kirkstone in her golden way was alluring; the mystery that shadowed the big house on the hill was fascinating to his hunting instincts; he had the desire, growing fast, to come at grips with Shan Tung. But he had not foreseen these things, and neither had Conniston foreseen them. They had planned only for the salvation of John Keith's precious neck, and tonight he had almost forgotten the existence of that unpleasant reality, the hangman. Truth settled upon him with depressing effect, and an infinite loneliness turned his mind again to the mountains of his dreams.

The town was empty of life. Lights glowed here and there through the mist; now and then a door opened; down near the river a dog howled forlornly. Everything was shut against him. There were no longer homes where he might call and be greeted with a cheery "Good evening, Keith. Glad to see you. Come in out of the wet." He could not even go to Duggan, his old river friend. He realized now that his old friends were the very ones he must avoid most carefully to escape self-betrayal. Friendship no longer existed for him; the town was a desert without an oasis where he might reclaim some of the things he had lost. Memories he had treasured gave place to bitter ones. His own townfolk, of all people, were his readiest enemies, and his loneliness clutched him tighter, until the air itself seemed thick and difficult to breathe. For the time Derwent Conniston was utterly submerged in the overwhelming yearnings of John Keith.

He dropped into a dimly lighted shop to purchase a box of cigars. It was deserted except for the proprietor. His elbow bumped into a telephone. He would call up Wallie and tell him to have a good fire waiting for him, and in the company of that fire he would do a lot of thinking before getting into communication with McDowell.

It was not Wallie who answered him, and he was about to apologize for getting the wrong number when the voice at the other end asked,

"Is that you, Conniston?"

It was McDowell. The discovery gave him a distinct shock. What could the Inspector be doing up at the Shack in his absence? Besides, there was an imperative demand in the question that shot at him over the wire. McDowell had half shouted it.

"Yes, it's I," he said rather feebly.

"I'm down-town, stocking up on some cigars. What's the excitement?"

"Don't ask questions but hustle up here," McDowell fired back. "I've got the surprise of your life waiting for you!"

Keith heard the receiver at the other end go up with a bang. Something had happened at the Shack, and McDowell was excited. He went out puzzled. For some reason he was in no great hurry to reach the top of the hill. He was beginning to expect things to happen—too many things—and in the stress of the moment he felt the incongruity of the friendly box of cigars tucked under his arm. The hardest luck he had ever run up against had never quite killed his sense of humor, and he chuckled. His fortunes were indeed at a low ebb when he found a bit of comfort in hugging a box of cigars still closer.

He could see that every room in the Shack was lighted, when he came to the crest of the slope, but the shades were drawn. He wondered if Wallie had pulled down the curtains, or if it was a caution on McDowell's part against possible espionage. Suspicion made him transfer the box of cigars to his left arm so that his right was free. Somewhere in the darkness Conniston's voice was urging him, as it had urged him up in the cabin on the Barren: "Don't walk into a noose. If it comes to a fight, FIGHT!"

And then something happened that brought his heart to a dead stop. He was close to the door. His ear was against it. And he was listening to a voice. It was not Wallie's, and it was not the iron man's. It was a woman's voice, or a girl's.

He opened the door and entered, taking swiftly the two or three steps that carried him across the tiny vestibule to the big room. His entrance was so sudden that the tableau in front of him was unbroken for a moment. Birch logs were blazing in the fireplace. In the big chair sat McDowell, partly turned, a smoking cigar poised in his fingers, staring at him. Seated on a footstool, with her chin in the cup of her hands, was a girl. At first, blinded a little by the light, Keith thought she was a child, a remarkably pretty child with wide-open, half-startled eyes and a wonderful crown of glowing, brown hair in which he could still see the shimmer of wet. He took off his hat and brushed the water from his eyes. McDowell did not move. Slowly the girl rose to her feet. It was then that Keith saw she was not a child. Perhaps she was eighteen, a slim, tired-looking, little thing, wonderfully pretty, and either on the verge of laughing or crying. Perhaps it was halfway between. To his growing discomfiture she came slowly toward him with a strange and wonderful look in her face. And McDowell still sat there staring.

His heart thumped with an emotion he had no time to question. In those wide-open, shining eyes of the girl he sensed unspeakable tragedy—for him. And then the girl's arms were reaching out to him, and she was crying in that voice that trembled and broke between sobs and laughter:

"Derry, don't you know me? Don't you know me?"

He stood like one upon whom had fallen the curse of the dumb. She was within arm's reach of him, her face white as a cameo, her eyes glowing like newly-fired stars, her slim throat quivering, and her arms reaching toward him.

"Derry, don't you know me? DON'T YOU KNOW ME?"

It was a sob, a cry. McDowell had risen. Overwhelmingly there swept upon Keith an impulse that rocked him to the depth of his soul. He opened his arms, and in an instant the girl was in them. Quivering, and sobbing, and laughing she was on his breast. He felt the crush of her soft hair against his face, her arms were about his neck, and she was pulling his head down and kissing him—not once or twice, but again and again, passionately and without shame. His own arms tightened. He heard McDowell's voice—a distant and non-essential voice it seemed to him now—saying that he would leave them alone and that he would see them again tomorrow. He heard the door open and close. McDowell was gone. And the soft little arms were still tight about his neck. The sweet crush of hair smothered his face, and on his breast she was crying now like a baby. He held her closer. A wild exultation seized upon him, and every fiber in his body responded to its thrill, as tautly-stretched wires respond to an electrical storm. It passed swiftly, burning itself out, and his heart was left dead. He heard a sound made by Wallie out in the kitchen. He saw the walls of the room again, the chair in which McDowell had sat, the blazing fire. His arms relaxed. The girl raised her head and put her two hands to his face, looking at him with eyes which Keith no longer failed to recognize. They were the eyes that had looked at him out of the faded picture in Conniston's watch.

"Kiss me, Derry!"

It was impossible not to obey. Her lips clung to him. There was love, adoration, in their caress.

And then she was crying again, with her arms around him tight and her face hidden against him, and he picked her up as he would have lifted a child, and carried her to the big chair in front of the fire. He put her in it and stood before her, trying to smile. Her hair had loosened, and the shining mass of it had fallen about her face and to her shoulders. She was more than ever like a little girl as she looked up at him, her eyes worshiping him, her lips trying to smile, and one little hand dabbing her eyes with a tiny handkerchief that was already wet and crushed.

"You—you don't seem very glad to see me, Derry."

"I—I'm just stunned," he managed to say. "You see—"

"It IS a shocking surprise, Derry. I meant it to be. I've been planning it for years and years and YEARS! Please take off your coat—it's dripping wet!—and sit down near me, on that stool!"

Again he obeyed. He was big for the stool.

"You are glad to see me, aren't you, Derry?"

She was leaning over the edge of the big chair, and one of her hands went to his damp hair, brushing it back. It was a wonderful touch. He had never felt anything like it before in his life, and involuntarily he bent his head a little. In a moment she had hugged it up close to her.

"You ARE glad, aren't you, Derry? Say 'yes.'"

"Yes," he whispered.

He could feel the swift, excited beating of her heart.

"And I'm never going back again—to THEM," he heard her say, something suddenly low and fierce in her voice. "NEVER! I'm going to stay with you always, Derry. Always!"

She put her lips close to his ear and whispered mysteriously. "They don't know where I am. Maybe they think I'm dead. But Colonel Reppington knows. I told him I was coming if I had to walk round the world to get here. He said he'd keep my secret, and gave me letters to some awfully nice people over here. I've been over six months. And when I saw your name in one of those dry-looking, blue-covered, paper books the Mounted Police get out, I just dropped down on my knees and thanked the good Lord, Derry. I knew I'd find you somewhere—sometime. I haven't slept two winks since leaving Montreal! And I guess I really frightened that big man with the terrible mustaches, for when I rushed in on him tonight, dripping wet, and said, 'I'm Miss Mary Josephine Conniston, and I want my brother,' his eyes grew bigger and bigger until I thought they were surely going to pop out at me. And then he swore. He said, 'My Gawd, I didn't know he had a sister!'"

Keith's heart was choking him. So this wonderful little creature was Derwent Conniston's sister! And she was claiming him. She thought he was her brother!

"—And I love him because he treated me so nicely," she was saying. "He really hugged me, Derry. I guess he didn't think I was away past eighteen. And he wrapped me up in a big oilskin, and we came up here. And—O Derry, Derry—why did you do it? Why didn't you let me know? Don't you—want me here?"

He heard, but his mind had swept beyond her to the little cabin in the edge of the Great Barren where Derwent Conniston lay dead. He heard the wind moaning, as it had moaned that night the Englishman died, and he saw again that last and unspoken yearning in Conniston's eyes. And he knew now why Conniston's face had followed him through the gray gloom and why he had felt the mysterious presence of him long after he had gone.

55

Something that was Conniston entered into him now. In the throbbing chaos of his brain a voice was whispering, "She is yours, she is yours."

His arms tightened about her, and a voice that was not unlike John Keith's voice said: "Yes, I want you! I want you!"

CHAPTER 10

For a space Keith did not raise his head. The girl's arms were about him close, and he could feel the warm pressure of her cheek against his hair. The realization of his crime was already weighing his soul like a piece of lead, yet out of that soul had come the cry, "I want you—I want you!" and it still beat with the voice of that immeasurable yearning even as his lips grew tight and he saw himself the monstrous fraud he was. This strange little, wonderful creature had come to him from out of a dead world, and her lips, and her arms, and the soft caress of her hands had sent his own world reeling about his head so swiftly that he had been drawn into a maelstrom to which he could find no bottom. Before McDowell she had claimed him. And before McDowell he had accepted her. He had lived the great lie as he had strengthened himself to live it, but success was no longer a triumph. There rushed into his brain like a consuming flame the desire to confess the truth, to tell this girl whose arms were about him that he was not Derwent Conniston, her brother, but John Keith, the murderer. Something drove it back, something that was still more potent, more demanding, the overwhelming urge of that fighting force in every man which calls for self-preservation.

Slowly he drew himself away from her, knowing that for this night at least his back was to the wall. She was smiling at him from out of the big chair, and in spite of himself he smiled back at her.

"I must send you to bed now, Mary Josephine, and tomorrow we will talk everything over," he said. "You're so tired you're ready to fall asleep in a minute."

Tiny, puckery lines came into her pretty forehead. It was a trick he loved at first sight.

"Do you know, Derry, I almost believe you've changed a lot. You used to call me 'Juddy.' But now that I'm grown up, I think I like Mary Josephine better, though you oughtn't to be quite so stiff about it. Derry, tell me honest—are you AFRAID of me?"

"Afraid of you!"

"Yes, because I'm grown up. Don't you like me as well as you did one, two, three, seven years ago? If you did, you wouldn't tell me to go to bed just a few minutes after you've seen me for the first time in all those—those—Derry, I'm going to cry! I AM!"

"Don't," he pleaded. "Please don't!"

57

He felt like a hundred-horned bull in a very small china shop. Mary Josephine herself saved the day for him by jumping suddenly from the big chair, forcing him into it, and snuggling herself on his knees.

"There!" She looked at a tiny watch on her wrist. "We're going to bed in two hours. We've got a lot to talk about that won't wait until tomorrow, Derry. You understand what I mean. I couldn't sleep until you've told me. And you must tell me the truth. I'll love you just the same, no matter what it is. Derry, Derry, WHY DID YOU DO IT?"

"Do what?" he asked stupidly.

The delicious softness went out of the slim little body on his knees. It grew rigid. He looked hopelessly into the fire, but he could feel the burning inquiry in the girl's eyes. He sensed a swift change passing through her. She seemed scarcely to breathe, and he knew that his answer had been more than inadequate. It either confessed or feigned an ignorance of something which it would have been impossible for him to forget had he been Conniston. He looked up at her at last. The joyous flush had gone out of her face. It was a little drawn. Her hand, which had been snuggling his neck caressingly, slipped down from his shoulder.

"I guess—you'd rather I hadn't come, Derry," she said, fighting to keep a break out of her voice. "And I'll go back, if you want to send me. But I've always dreamed of your promise, that some day you'd send for me or come and get me, and I'd like to know WHY before you tell me to go. Why have you hidden away from me all these years, leaving me among those who you knew hated me as they hated you? Was it because you didn't care? Or was it because—because—" She bent her head and whispered strangely, "Was it because you were afraid?"

"Afraid?" he repeated slowly, staring again into the fire. "Afraid—" He was going to add "Of what?" but caught the words and held them back.

The birch fire leaped up with a sudden roar into the chimney, and from the heart of the flame he caught again that strange and all-pervading thrill, the sensation of Derwent Conniston's presence very near to him. It seemed to him that for an instant he caught a flash of Conniston's face, and somewhere within him was a whispering which was Conniston's voice. He was possessed by a weird and masterful force that swept over him and conquered him, a thing that was more than intuition and greater than physical desire. It was inspiration. He knew that the Englishman would have him play the game as he was about to play it now.

The girl was waiting for him to answer. Her lips had grown a little more tense. His hesitation, the restraint in his welcome of her, and his apparent desire to evade that mysterious something which seemed to mean so much to her had brought a shining pain into her eyes. He had seen such a look in the eyes of creatures physically hurt. He reached out with his hands and brushed back the thick, soft hair from about her face. His fingers buried themselves in the silken disarray, and he looked for a moment straight into her eyes before he spoke.

"Little girl, will you tell me the truth?" he asked. "Do I look like the old Derwent Conniston, YOUR Derwent Conniston? Do I?"

Her voice was small and troubled, yet the pain was slowly fading out of her eyes as she felt the passionate embrace of his fingers in her hair. "No. You are changed."

"Yes, I am changed. A part of Derwent Conniston died seven years ago. That part of him was dead until he came through that door tonight and saw you. And then it flickered back into life. It is returning slowly, slowly. That which was dead is beginning to rouse itself, beginning to remember. See, little Mary Josephine. It was this!"

He drew a hand to his forehead and placed a finger on the scar. "I got that seven years ago. It killed a half of Derwent Conniston, the part that should have lived. Do you understand? Until tonight—"

Her eyes startled him, they were growing so big and dark and staring, living fires of understanding and horror. It was hard for him to go on with the lie. "For many weeks I was dead," he struggled on. "And when I came to life physically, I had forgotten a great deal. I had my name, my identity, but only ghastly dreams and visions of what had gone before. I remembered you, but it was in a dream, a strange and haunting dream that was with me always. It seems to me that for an age I have been seeking for a face, a voice, something I loved above all else on earth, something which was always near and yet was never found. It was you, Mary Josephine, you!"

Was it the real Derwent Conniston speaking now? He felt again that overwhelming force from within which was not his own. The thing that had begun as a lie struck him now as a thing that was truth. It was he, John Keith, who had been questing and yearning and hoping. It was John Keith, and not Conniston, who had returned into a world filled with a desolation of loneliness, and it was to John Keith that a beneficent God had sent this wonderful creature in an hour that was blackest in its despair. He was not lying now. He was fighting. He was fighting to keep for himself the one atom of humanity that meant more to him than all the rest of the human race, fighting to keep a great love that had come to him out of a world in which he no longer had a friend or a home, and to that fight his soul went

59

out as a drowning man grips at a spar on a sea. As the girl's hands came to his face and he heard the yearning, grief-filled cry of his name on her lips, he no longer sensed the things he was saying, but held her close in his arms, kissing her mouth, and her eyes, and her hair, and repeating over and over again that now he had found her he would never give her up. Her arms clung to him. They were like two children brought together after a long separation, and Keith knew that Conniston's love for this girl who was his sister must have been a splendid thing. And his lie had saved Conniston as well as himself. There had been no time to question the reason for the Englishman's neglect—for his apparent desertion of the girl who had come across the sea to find him. Tonight it was sufficient that HE was Conniston, and that to him the girl had fallen as a precious heritage.

He stood up with her at last, holding her away from him a little so that he could look into her face wet with tears and shining with happiness. She reached up a hand to his face, so that it touched the scar, and in her eyes he saw an infinite pity, a luminously tender glow of love and sympathy and understanding that no measurements could compass. Gently her hand stroked his scarred forehead. He felt his old world slipping away from under his feet, and with his triumph there surged over him a thankfulness for that indefinable something that had come to him in time to give him the strength and the courage to lie. For she believed him, utterly and without the shadow of a suspicion she believed him.

"Tomorrow you will help me to remember a great many things," he said. "And now will you let me send you to bed, Mary Josephine?"

She was looking at the scar. "And all those years I didn't know," she whispered. "I didn't know. They told me you were dead, but I knew it was a lie. It was Colonel Reppington—" She saw something in his face that stopped her.

"Derry, DON'T YOU REMEMBER?"

"I shall—tomorrow. But tonight I can see nothing and think of nothing but you. Tomorrow—"

She drew his head down swiftly and kissed the brand made by the heated barrel of the Englishman's pistol. "Yes, yes, we must go to bed now, Derry," she cried quickly. "You must not think too much. Tonight it must just be of me. Tomorrow everything will come out right, everything. And now you may send me to bed. Do you remember—"

She caught herself, biting her lip to keep back the word.

"Tell me," he urged. "Do I remember what?"

"How you used to come in at the very last and tuck me in at night, Derry? And how we used to whisper to ourselves there in the darkness, and at last you would kiss me good-night? It was the kiss that always made me go to sleep."

He nodded. "Yes, I remember," he said.

He led her to the spare room, and brought in her two travel-worn bags, and turned on the light. It was a man's room, but Mary Josephine stood for a moment surveying it with delight.

"It's home, Derry, real home," she whispered.

He did not explain to her that it was a borrowed home and that this was his first night in it. Such unimportant details would rest until tomorrow. He showed her the bath and its water system and then explained to Wallie that his sister was in the house and he would have to bunk in the kitchen. At the last he knew what he was expected to do, what he must do. He kissed Mary Josephine good night. He kissed her twice. And Mary Josephine kissed him and gave him a hug the like of which he had never experienced until this night. It sent him back to the fire with blood that danced like a drunken man's.

He turned the lights out and for an hour sat in the dying glow of the birch. For the first time since he had come from Miriam Kirkstone's he had the opportunity to think, and in thinking he found his brain crowded with cold and unemotional fact. He saw his lie in all its naked immensity. Yet he was not sorry that he had lied. He had saved Conniston. He had saved himself. And he had saved Conniston's sister, to love, to fight for, to protect. It had not been a Judas lie but a lie with his heart and his soul and all the manhood in him behind it. To have told the truth would have made him his own executioner, it would have betrayed the dead Englishman who had given to him his name and all that he possessed, and it would have dragged to a pitiless grief the heart of a girl for whom the sun still continued to shine. No regret rose before him now. He felt no shame. All that he saw was the fight, the tremendous fight, ahead of him, his fight to make good as Conniston, his fight to play the game as Conniston would have him play it. The inspiration that had come to him as he stood facing the storm from the western mountains possessed him again. He would go to the river's end as he had planned to go before McDowell told him of Shan Tung and Miriam Kirkstone. And he would not go alone. Mary Josephine would go with him.

It was midnight when he rose from the big chair and went to his room. The door was closed. He opened it and entered. Even as his hand groped for the switch on the wall, his nostrils caught the scent of something which was familiar and yet which should not have been there. It filled the room, just as it had filled the big hall at the Kirkstone house, the almost sickening fragrance of agallochum burned in a cigarette. It hung like a heavy incense. Keith's eyes glared as he scanned the room under the lights, half expecting to see Shan Tung sitting there waiting for him. It was empty. His eyes leaped to the two windows. The shade was drawn at one, the other was up, and the window itself was open an inch or two above the sill. Keith's hand gripped his pistol as he went to it and drew the curtain. Then he turned to the table on which were the reading lamp and Brady's pipes and tobacco and magazines. On an ash-tray lay the stub of a freshly burned cigarette. Shan Tung had come secretly, but he had made no effort to cover his presence.

It was then that Keith saw something on the table which had not been there before. It was a small, rectangular, teakwood box no larger than a half of the palm of his hand. He had noticed Miriam Kirkstone's nervous fingers toying with just such a box earlier in the evening. They were identical in appearance. Both were covered with an exquisite fabric of oriental carving, and the wood was stained and polished until it shone with the dark luster of ebony. Instantly it flashed upon him that this was the same box he had seen at Miriam's. She had sent it to him, and Shan Tung had been her messenger. The absurd thought was in his head as he took up a small white square of card that lay on top of the box. The upper side of this card was blank; on the other side, in a script as exquisite in its delicacy as the carving itself, were the words:

"WITH THE COMPLIMENTS OF SHAN TUNG."

In another moment Keith had opened the box. Inside was a carefully folded slip of paper, and on this paper was written a single line. Keith's heart stopped beating, and his blood ran cold as he read what it held for him, a message of doom from Shan Tung in nine words:

"WHAT HAPPENED TO DERWENT CONNISTON? DID YOU KILL HIM?"

CHAPTER 11

Stunned by a shock that for a few moments paralyzed every nerve center in his body, John Keith stood with the slip of white paper in his hands. He was discovered! That was the one thought that pounded like a hammer in his brain. He was discovered in the very hour of his triumph and exaltation, in that hour when the world had opened its portals of joy and hope for him again and when life itself, after four years of hell, was once more worth the living. Had the shock come a few hours before, he would have taken it differently. He was expecting it then. He had expected it when he entered McDowell's office the first time. He was prepared for it afterward. Discovery, failure, and death were possibilities of the hazardous game he was playing, and he was unafraid, because he had only his life to lose, a life that was not much more than a hopeless derelict at most. Now it was different. Mary Josephine had come like some rare and wonderful alchemy to transmute for him all leaden things into gold. In a few minutes she had upset the world. She had literally torn aside for him the hopeless chaos in which he saw himself struggling, flooding him with the warm radiance of a great love and a still greater desire. On his lips he could feel the soft thrill of her good-night kiss and about his neck the embrace of her soft arms. She had not gone to sleep yet. Across in the other room she was thinking of him, loving him; perhaps she was on her knees praying for him, even as he held in his fingers Shan Tung's mysterious forewarning of his doom.

The first impulse that crowded in upon him was that of flight, the selfish impulse of personal salvation. He could get away. The night would swallow him up. A moment later he was mentally castigating himself for the treachery of that impulse to Mary Josephine. His floundering senses began to readjust themselves.

Why had Shan Tung given him this warning? Why had he not gone straight to Inspector McDowell with the astounding disclosure of the fact that the man supposed to be Derwent Conniston was not Derwent Conniston, but John Keith, the murderer of Miriam Kirkstone's father?

The questions brought to Keith a new thrill. He read the note again. It was a definite thing stating a certainty and not a guess. Shan Tung had not shot at random. He knew. He knew that he was not Derwent Conniston but John Keith. And he believed that he had killed the Englishman to steal his identity. In the face of these things he had not gone to McDowell! Keith's eyes fell upon the card again. "With the compliments of Shan Tung." What did the words mean? Why had Shan Tung written them unless—with his compliments—he was giving him a warning and the chance to save himself?

His immediate alarm grew less. The longer he contemplated the slip of paper in his hand, the more he became convinced that the inscrutable Shan Tung was the last individual in the world to stage a bit of melodrama without some good reason for it. There was but one conclusion he could arrive at. The Chinaman was playing a game of his own, and he had taken this unusual way of advising Keith to make a getaway while the going was good. It was evident that his intention had been to avoid the possibility of a personal discussion of the situation. That, at least, was Keith's first impression.

He turned to examine the window. There was no doubt that Shan Tung had come in that way. Both the sill and curtain bore stains of water and mud, and there was wet dirt on the floor. For once the immaculate oriental had paid no attention to his feet. At the door leading into the big room Keith saw where he had stood for some time, listening, probably when McDowell and Mary Josephine were in the outer room waiting for him. Suddenly his eyes riveted themselves on the middle panel of the door. Brady had intended his color scheme to be old ivory—the panel itself was nearly white—and on it Shan Tung had written heavily with a lead pencil the hour of his presence, "10.45 P.M." Keith's amazement found voice in a low exclamation. He looked at his watch. It was a quarter-hour after twelve. He had returned to the Shack before ten, and the clever Shan Tung was letting him know in this cryptic fashion that for more than three-quarters of an hour he had listened at the door and spied upon him and Mary Josephine through the keyhole.

Had even such an insignificant person as Wallie been guilty of that act, Keith would have felt like thrashing him. It surprised himself that he experienced no personal feeling of outrage at Shan Tung's frank confession of eavesdropping. A subtle significance began to attach itself more and more to the story his room was telling him. He knew that Shan Tung had left none of the marks of his presence out of bravado, but with a definite purpose. Keith's psychological mind was at all times acutely ready to seize upon possibilities, and just as his positiveness of Conniston's spiritual presence had inspired him to act his lie with Mary Josephine, so did the conviction possess him now that his room held for him a message of the most vital importance.

In such an emergency Keith employed his own method. He sat down, lighted his pipe again, and centered the full resource of his mind on Shan Tung, dissociating himself from the room and the adventure of the night as much as possible in his objective analysis of the man. Four distinct emotional factors entered into that analysis—fear, distrust, hatred, personal enmity. To his surprise he found himself drifting steadily into an unusual and unexpected mental attitude. From the time he had faced Shan Tung in the inspector's office, he had regarded him as the chief enemy of his freedom, his one great menace. Now he felt neither personal enmity nor hatred for him. Fear and distrust remained, but the fear was impersonal and the distrust that of one who watches a clever opponent in a game or a fight. His conception of Shan Tung changed. He found his occidental mind running parallel with the oriental, bridging the spaces which otherwise it never would have crossed, and at the end it seized upon the key. It proved to him that his first impulse had been wrong. Shan Tung had not expected him to seek safety in flight. He had given the white man credit for a larger understanding than that. His desire, first of all, had been to let Keith know that he was not the only one who was playing for big stakes, and that another, Shan Tung himself, was gambling a hazard of his own, and that the fraudulent Derwent Conniston was a trump card in that game.

To impress this upon Keith he had, first of all, acquainted him with the fact that he had seen through his deception and that he knew he was John Keith and not Derwent Conniston. He had also let him know that he believed he had killed the Englishman, a logical supposition under the circumstances. This information he had left for Keith was not in the form of an intimidation. There was, indeed, something very near apologetic courtesy in the presence of the card bearing Shan Tung's compliments. The penciling of the hour on the panel of the door, without other notation, was a polite and suggestive hint. He wanted Keith to know that he understood his peculiar situation up until that particular time, that he had heard and possibly seen much that had passed between him and Mary Josephine. The partly opened window, the mud and wet on curtains and floor, and the cigarette stubs were all to call Keith's attention to the box on the table.

Keith could not but feel a certain sort of admiration for the Chinaman. The two questions he must answer now were, What was Shan Tung's game? and What did Shan Tung expect him to do?

Instantly Miriam Kirkstone flashed upon him as the possible motive for Shan Tung's visit. He recalled her unexpected and embarrassing question of that evening, in which she had expressed a suspicion and a doubt as to John

Keith's death. He had gone to Miriam's at eight. It must have been very soon after that, and after she had caught a glimpse of the face at the window, that Shan Tung had hurried to the Shack.

Slowly but surely the tangled threads of the night's adventure were unraveling themselves for Keith. The main facts pressed upon him, no longer smothered in a chaos of theory and supposition. If there had been no Miriam Kirkstone in the big house on the hill, Shan Tung would have gone to McDowell, and he would have been in irons at the present moment. McDowell had been right after all. Miriam Kirkstone was fighting for something that was more than her existence. The thought of that "something" made Keith writhe and his hands clench. Shan Tung had triumphed but not utterly. A part of the fruit of his triumph was still just out of his reach, and the two—beautiful Miss Kirkstone and the deadly Shan Tung—were locked in a final struggle for its possession. In some mysterious way he, John Keith, was to play the winning hand. How or when he could not understand. But of one thing he was convinced; in exchange for whatever winning card he held Shan Tung had offered him his life. Tomorrow he would expect an answer.

That tomorrow had already dawned. It was one o'clock when Keith again looked at his watch. Twenty hours ago he had cooked his last camp-fire breakfast. It was only eighteen hours ago that he had filled himself with the smell of Andy Duggan's bacon, and still more recently that he had sat in the little barber shop on the corner wondering what his fate would be when he faced McDowell. It struck him as incongruous and impossible that only fifteen hours had passed since then. If he possessed a doubt of the reality of it all, the bed was there to help convince him. It was a real bed, and he had not slept in a real bed for a number of years. Wallie had made it ready for him. Its sheets were snow-white. There was a counterpane with a fringe on it and pillows puffed up with billowy invitation, as if they were on the point of floating away. Had they risen before his eyes, Keith would have regarded the phenomenon rather casually. After the swift piling up of the amazing events of those fifteen hours, a floating pillow would have seemed quite in the natural orbit of things. But they did not float. They remained where they were, their white breasts bared to him, urging upon him a common-sense perspective of the situation. He wasn't going to run away. He couldn't sit up all night. Therefore why not come to them and sleep?

There was something directly personal in the appeal of the pillows and the bed. It was not general; it was for him. And Keith responded.

He made another note of the time, a half-hour after one, when he turned in. He allotted himself four hours of sleep, for it was his intention to be up with the sun.

CHAPTER 12

Necessity had made of Keith a fairly accurate human chronometer. In the second year of his fugitivism he had lost his watch. At first it was like losing an arm, a part of his brain, a living friend. From that time until he came into possession of Conniston's timepiece he was his own hour-glass and his own alarm clock. He became proficient.

Brady's bed and the Circe-breasted pillows that supported his head were his undoing. The morning after Shan Tung's visit he awoke to find the sun flooding in through the eastern window of his room, The warmth of it as it fell full in his face, setting his eyes blinking, told him it was too late. He guessed it was eight o'clock. When he fumbled his watch out from under his pillow and looked at it, he found it was a quarter past. He got up quietly, his mind swiftly aligning itself to the happenings of yesterday. He stretched himself until his muscles snapped, and his chest expanded with deep breaths of air from the windows he had left open when he went to bed. He was fit. He was ready for Shan Tung, for McDowell. And over this physical readiness there surged the thrill of a glorious anticipation. It fairly staggered him to discover how badly he wanted to see Mary Josephine again.

He wondered if she was still asleep and answered that there was little possibility of her being awake—even at eight o'clock. Probably she would sleep until noon, the poor, tired, little thing! He smiled affectionately into the mirror over Brady's dressing-table. And then the unmistakable sound of voices in the outer room took him curiously to the door. They were subdued voices. He listened hard, and his heart pumped faster. One of them was Wallie's voice; the other was Mary Josephine's.

He was amused with himself at the extreme care with which he proceeded to dress. It was an entirely new sensation. Wallie had provided him with the necessaries for a cold sponge and in some mysterious interim since their arrival had brushed and pressed the most important of Conniston's things. With the Englishman's wardrobe he had brought up from barracks a small chest which was still locked. Until this morning Keith had not noticed it. It was less than half as large as a steamer trunk and had the appearance of being intended as a strong box rather than a traveling receptacle. It was ribbed by four heavy bands of copper, and the corners and edges were reinforced with the same metal. The lock itself seemed to be impregnable to one without a key. Conniston's name was heavily engraved on a copper tablet just above the lock.

Keith regarded the chest with swiftly growing speculation. It was not a thing one would ordinarily possess. It was an object which, on the face of it, was intended to be inviolate except to its master key, a holder of treasure, a guardian of mystery and of precious secrets. In the little cabin up on the Barren Conniston had said rather indifferently, "You may find something among my things down there that will help you out." The words flashed back to Keith. Had the Englishman, in that casual and uncommunicative way of his, referred to the contents of this chest? Was it not possible that it held for him a solution to the mystery that was facing him in the presence of Mary Josephine? A sense of conviction began to possess him. He examined the lock more closely and found that with proper tools it could be broken.

He finished dressing and completed his toilet by brushing his beard. On account of Mary Josephine he found himself regarding this hirsute tragedy with a growing feeling of disgust, in spite of the fact that it gave him an appearance rather distinguished and military. He wanted it off. Its chief crime was that it made him look older. Besides, it was inclined to be reddish. And it must tickle and prick like the deuce when—

He brought himself suddenly to salute with an appreciative grin. "You're there, and you've got to stick," he chuckled. After all, he was a likable-looking chap, even with that handicap. He was glad.

He opened his door so quietly that Mary Josephine did not see him at first. Her back was toward him as she bent over the dining-table. Her slim little figure was dressed in some soft stuff all crinkly from packing. Her hair, brown and soft, was piled up in shining coils on the top of her head. For the life of him Keith couldn't keep his eyes from traveling from the top of that glowing head to the little high-heeled feet on the floor. They were adorable, slim little, aristocratic feet with dainty ankles! He stood looking at her until she turned and caught him.

There was a change since last night. She was older. He could see it now, the utter impropriety of his cuddling her up like a baby in the big chair—the impossibility, almost.

Mary Josephine settled his doubt. With a happy little cry she ran to him, and Keith found her arms about him again and her lovely mouth held up to be kissed. He hesitated for perhaps the tenth part of a second, if hesitation could be counted in that space. Then his arms closed about her, and he kissed her. He felt the snuggle of her face against his breast again, the crush and sweetness of her hair against his lips and cheek. He kissed her again uninvited. Before he could stop the habit, he had kissed her a third time.

Then her hands were at his face, and he saw again that look in her eyes, a deep and anxious questioning behind the shimmer of love in them, something mute and understanding and wonderfully sympathetic, a mothering soul looking at him and praying as it looked. If his life had paid the forfeit the next instant, he could not have helped kissing her a fourth time.

If Mary Josephine had gone to bed with a doubt of his brotherly interest last night, the doubt was removed now. Her cheeks flushed. Her eyes shone. She was palpitantly, excitedly happy. "It's YOU, Derry," she cried. "Oh, it's you as you used to be!"

She seized his hand and drew him toward the table. Wallie thrust in his head from the kitchenette, grinning, and Mary Josephine flashed him back a meaning smile. Keith saw in an instant that Wallie had turned from his heathen gods to the worship of something infinitely more beautiful. He no longer looked to Keith for instructions.

Mary Josephine sat down opposite Keith at the table. She was telling him, with that warm laughter and happiness in her eyes, how the sun had wakened her, and how she had helped Wallie get breakfast. For the first time Keith was looking at her from a point of vantage; there was just so much distance between them, no more and no less, and the light was right. She was, to him, exquisite. The little puckery lines came into her smooth forehead when he apologized for his tardiness by explaining that he had not gone to bed until one o'clock. Her concern was delightful. She scolded him while Wallie brought in the breakfast, and inwardly he swelled with the irrepressible exultation of a great possessor. He had never had anyone to scold him like that before. It was a scolding which expressed Mary Josephine's immediate proprietorship of him, and he wondered if the pleasure of it made him look as silly as Wallie. His plans were all gone. He had intended to play the idiotic part of one who had partly lost his memory, but throughout the breakfast he exhibited no sign that he was anything but healthfully normal. Mary Josephine's delight at the improvement of his condition since last night shone in her face and eyes, and he could see that she was strictly, but with apparent unconsciousness, guarding herself against saying anything that might bring up the dread shadow between them. She had already begun to fight her own fight for him, and the thing was so beautiful that he wanted to go round to her, and get down on his knees, and put his head in her lap, and tell her the truth.

It was in the moment of that thought that the look came into his face which brought the questioning little lines into her forehead again. In that

70

instant she caught a glimpse of the hunted man, of the soul that had traded itself, of desire beaten into helplessness by a thing she would never understand. It was gone swiftly, but she had caught it. And for her the scar just under his hair stood for its meaning. The responsive throb in her breast was electric. He felt it, saw it, sensed it to the depth of his soul, and his faith in himself stood challenged. She believed. And he—was a liar. Yet what a wonderful thing to lie for!

"—He called me up over the telephone, and when I told him to be quiet, that you were still asleep, I think he must have sworn—it sounded like it, but I couldn't hear distinctly—and then he fairly roared at me to wake you up and tell you that you didn't half deserve such a lovely little sister as I am. Wasn't that nice, Derry?"

"You—you're talking about McDowell?"

"To be sure I am talking about Mr. McDowell! And when I told him your injury troubled you more than usual, and that I was glad you were resting, I think I heard him swallow hard. He thinks a lot of you, Derry. And then he asked me WHICH injury it was that hurt you, and I told him the one in the head. What did he mean? Were you hurt somewhere else, Derry?"

Keith swallowed hard, too. "Not to speak of," he said. "You see, Mary Josephine, I've got a tremendous surprise for you, if you'll promise it won't spoil your appetite. Last night was the first night I've spent in a real bed for three years."

And then, without waiting for her questions, he began to tell her the epic story of John Keith. With her sitting opposite him, her beautiful, wide-open, gray eyes looking at him with amazement as she sensed the marvelous coincidence of their meeting, he told it as he had not told it to McDowell or even to Miriam Kirkstone. A third time the facts were the same. But it was John Keith now who was telling John Keith's story through the lips of an unreal and negative Conniston. He forgot his own breakfast, and a look of gloom settled on Wallie's face when he peered in through the door and saw that their coffee and toast were growing cold. Mary Josephine leaned a little over the table. Not once did she interrupt Keith. Never had he dreamed of a glory that might reflect his emotions as did her eyes. As he swept from pathos to storm, from the madness of long, black nights to starvation and cold, as he told of flight, of pursuit, of the merciless struggle that ended at last in the capture of John Keith, as he gave to these things words and life pulsing with the beat of his own heart, he saw them revisioned in those wonderful gray eyes, cold at times with fear, warm and glowing at other

71

times with sympathy, and again shining softly with a glory of pride and love that was meant for him alone. With him she was present in the little cabin up in the big Barren. Until he told of those days and nights of hopeless desolation, of racking cough and the nearness of death, and of the comradeship of brothers that had come as a final benediction to the hunter and the hunted, until in her soul she was understanding and living those terrible hours as they two had lived them, he did not know how deep and dark and immeasurably tender that gray mystery of beauty in her eyes could be. From that hour he worshiped them as he worshiped no other part of her.

"And from all that you came back the same day I came," she said in a low, awed voice. "You came back from THAT!"

He remembered the part he must play.

"Yes, three years of it. If I could only remember as well, only half as well, things that happened before this—" He raised a hand to his forehead, to the scar.

"You will," she whispered swiftly. "Derry, darling, you will!"

Wallie sidled in and, with an adoring grin at Mary Josephine, suggested that he had more coffee and toast ready to serve, piping hot. Keith was relieved. The day had begun auspiciously, and over the bacon and eggs, done to a ravishing brown by the little Jap, he told Mary Josephine of some of his bills of fare in the north and how yesterday he had filled up on bacon smell at Andy Duggan's. Steak from the cheek of a walrus, he told her, was equal to porterhouse; seal meat wasn't bad, but one grew tired of it quickly unless he was an Eskimo; polar bear meat was filling but tough and strong. He liked whale meat, especially the tail-steaks of narwhal, and cold boiled blubber was good in the winter, only it was impossible to cook it because of lack of fuel, unless one was aboard ship or had an alcohol stove in his outfit. The tidbit of the Eskimo was birds' eggs, gathered by the ton in summer-time, rotten before cold weather came, and frozen solid as chunks of ice in winter. Through one starvation period of three weeks he had lived on them himself, crunching them raw in his mouth as one worries away with a piece of rock candy. The little lines gathered in Mary Josephine's forehead at this, but they smoothed away into laughter when he humorously described the joy of living on nothing at all but air. And he added to this by telling her how the gluttonous Eskimo at feast-time would lie out flat on their backs so that their womenfolk could feed them by dropping chunks of flesh into their open maws until their stomachs swelled up like the crops of birds overstuffed with grain.

It was a successful breakfast. When it was over, Keith felt that he had achieved a great deal. Before they rose from the table, he startled Mary Josephine by ordering Wallie to bring him a cold chisel and a hammer from Brady's tool-chest.

"I've lost the key that opens my chest, and I've got to break in," he explained to her.

Mary Josephine's little laugh was delicious. "After what you told me about frozen eggs, I thought perhaps you were going to eat some," she said.

She linked her arm in his as they walked into the big room, snuggling her head against his shoulder so that, leaning over, his lips were buried in one of the soft, shining coils of her hair. And she was making plans, enumerating them on the tips of her fingers. If he had business outside, she was going with him. Wherever he went she was going. There was no doubt in her mind about that. She called his attention to a trunk that had arrived while he slept, and assured him she would be ready for outdoors by the time he had opened his chest. She had a little blue suit she was going to wear. And her hair? Did it look good enough for his friends to see? She had put it up in a hurry.

"It is beautiful, glorious," he said.

Her face pinked under the ardency of his gaze. She put a finger to the tip of his nose, laughing at him. "Why, Derry, if you weren't my brother I'd think you were my lover! You said that as though you meant it TERRIBLY much. Do you?"

He felt a sudden dull stab of pain, "Yes, I mean it. It's glorious. And so are you, Mary Josephine, every bit of you."

On tiptoe she gave him the warm sweetness of her lips again. And then she ran away from him, joy and laughter in her face, and disappeared into her room. "You must hurry or I shall beat you," she called back to him.

CHAPTER 13

In his own room, with the door closed and locked, Keith felt again that dull, strange pain that made his heart sick and the air about him difficult to breathe.

"IF YOU WEREN'T MY BROTHER."

The words beat in his brain. They were pounding at his heart until it was smothered, laughing at him and taunting him and triumphing over him just as, many times before, the raving voices of the weird wind-devils had scourged him from out of black night and arctic storm. HER BROTHER! His hand clenched until the nails bit into his flesh. No, he hadn't thought of that part of the fight! And now it swept upon him in a deluge. If he lost in the fight that was ahead of him, his life would pay the forfeit. The law would take him, and he would hang. And if he won—she would be his sister forever and to the end of all time! Just that, and no more. His SISTER! And the agony of truth gripped him that it was not as a brother that he saw the glory in her hair, the glory in her eyes and face, and the glory in her slim little, beautiful body—but as the lover. A merciless preordination had stacked the cards against him again. He was Conniston, and she was Conniston's sister.

A strong man, a man in whom blood ran red, there leaped up in him for a moment a sudden and unreasoning rage at that thing which he had called fate. He saw the unfairness of it all, the hopelessness of it, the cowardly subterfuge and trickery of life itself as it had played against him, and with tightly set lips and clenched hands he called mutely on God Almighty to play the game square. Give him a chance! Give him just one square deal, only one; let him see a way, let him fight a man's fight with a ray of hope ahead! In these red moments hope emblazoned itself before his eyes as a monstrous lie. Bitterness rose in him until he was drunk with it, and blasphemy filled his heart. Whichever way he turned, however hard he fought, there was no chance of winning. From the day he killed Kirkstone the cards had been stacked against him, and they were stacked now and would be stacked until the end. He had believed in God, he had believed in the inevitable ethics of the final reckoning of things, and he had believed strongly that an impersonal Something more powerful than man-made will was behind him in his struggles. These beliefs were smashed now. Toward them he felt the impulse of a maddened beast trampling hated things under foot. They stood for lies—treachery—cheating—yes, contemptible cheating! It was impossible for him to win. However he played, whichever way he turned, he must lose. For he was Conniston, and she was Conniston's sister, AND MUST BE TO THE END OF TIME.

Faintly, beyond the door, he heard Mary Josephine singing. Like a bit of steel drawn to a tension his normal self snapped back into place. His readjustment came with a lurch, a subtle sort of shock. His hands unclenched, the tense lines in his face relaxed, and because that God Almighty he had challenged had given to him an unquenchable humor, he saw another thing where only smirking ghouls and hypocrites had rent his brain with their fiendish exultations a moment before. It was Conniston's face, suave, smiling, dying, triumphant over life, and Conniston was saying, just as he had said up there in the cabin on the Barren, with death reaching out a hand for him, "It's queer, old top, devilish queer—and funny!"

Yes, it was funny if one looked at it right, and Keith found himself swinging back into his old view-point. It was the hugest joke life had ever played on him. His sister! He could fancy Conniston twisting his mustaches, his cool eyes glimmering with silent laughter, looking on his predicament, and he could fancy Conniston saying: "It's funny, old top, devilish funny—but it'll be funnier still when some other man comes along and carries her off!"

And he, John Keith, would have to grin and bear it because he was her brother!

Mary Josephine was tapping at his door.

"Derwent Conniston," she called frigidly, "there's a female person on the telephone asking for you. What shall I say?"

"Er—why—tell her you're my sister, Mary Josephine, and if it's Miss Kirkstone, be nice to her and say I'm not able to come to the 'phone, and that you're looking forward to meeting her, and that we'll be up to see her some time today."

"Oh, indeed!"

"You see," said Keith, his mouth close to the door, "you see, this Miss Kirkstone—"

But Mary Josephine was gone.

Keith grinned. His illimitable optimism was returning. Sufficient for the day that she was there, that she loved him, that she belonged to him, that just now he was the arbiter of her destiny! Far off in the mountains he dreamed of, alone, just they two, what might not happen? Some day—

With the cold chisel and the hammer he went to the chest. His task was one that numbed his hands before the last of the three locks was broken. He dragged the chest more into the light and opened it. He was disappointed. At first glance he could not understand why Conniston had locked it at all. It was almost empty, so nearly empty that he could see the bottom of it, and the first object that met his eyes was an insult to his expectations—an old sock with a huge hole in the toe of it. Under the sock was an old fur cap not of the kind worn north of Montreal. There was a chain with a dog-collar attached to it, a hip-pocket pistol and a huge forty-five, and not less than a hundred cartridges of indiscriminate calibers scattered loosely about. At one end, bundled in carelessly, was a pair of riding-breeches, and under the breeches a pair of white shoes with rubber soles. There was neither sentiment nor reason to the collection in the chest. It was junk. Even the big forty-five had a broken hammer, and the pistol, Keith thought, might have stunned a fly at close range. He pawed the things over with the cold chisel, and the last thing he came upon—buried under what looked like a cast-off sport shirt—was a pasteboard shoe box. He raised the cover. The box was full of papers.

Here was promise. He transported the box to Brady's table and sat down. He examined the larger papers first. There were a couple of old game licenses for Manitoba, half a dozen pencil-marked maps, chiefly of the Peace River country, and a number of letters from the secretaries of Boards of Trade pointing out the incomparable possibilities their respective districts held for the homesteader and the buyer of land. Last of all came a number of newspaper clippings and a packet of letters.

Because they were loose he seized upon the clippings first, and as his eyes fell upon the first paragraph of the first clipping his body became suddenly tensed in the shock of unexpected discovery and amazed interest. There were six of the clippings, all from English papers, English in their terseness, brief as stock exchange reports, and equally to the point. He read the six in three minutes.

They simply stated that Derwent Conniston, of the Connistons of Darlington, was wanted for burglary—and that up to date he had not been found.

Keith gave a gasp of incredulity. He looked again to see that his eyes were not tricking him. And it was there in cold, implacable print. Derwent Conniston—that phoenix among men, by whom he had come to measure all other men, that Crichton of nerve, of calm and audacious courage, of splendid poise—a burglar! It was cheap, farcical, an impossible absurdity. Had it been murder, high treason, defiance of some great law, a great crime inspired by a great passion or a great ideal, but it was burglary, brigandage

76

of the cheapest and most commonplace variety, a sneaking night-coward's plagiarism of real adventure and real crime. It was impossible. Keith gritted the words aloud. He might have accepted Conniston as a Dick Turpin, a Claude Duval or a Macheath, but not as a Jeremy Diddler or a Bill Sykes. The printed lines were lies. They must be. Derwent Conniston might have killed a dozen men, but he had never cracked a safe. To think it was to think the inconceivable.

He turned to the letters. They were postmarked Darlington, England. His fingers tingled as he opened the first. It was as he had expected, as he had hoped. They were from Mary Josephine. He arranged them—nine in all—in the sequence of their dates, which ran back nearly eight years. All of them had been written within a period of eleven months. They were as legible as print. And as he passed from the first to the second, and from the second to the third, and then read on into the others, he forgot there was such a thing as time and that Mary Josephine was waiting for him. The clippings had told him one thing; here, like bits of driftage to be put together, a line in this place and half a dozen in that, in paragraphs that enlightened and in others that puzzled, was the other side of the story, a growing thing that rose up out of mystery and doubt in segments and fractions of segments adding themselves together piecemeal, welding the whole into form and substance, until there rode through Keith's veins a wild thrill of exultation and triumph.

And then he came to the ninth and last letter. It was in a different handwriting, brief, with a deadly specificness about it that gripped Keith as he read.

This ninth letter he held in his hand as he rose from the table, and out of his mouth there fell, unconsciously, Conniston's own words, "It's devilish queer, old top—and funny!"

There was no humor in the way he spoke them. His voice was hard, his eyes dully ablaze. He was looking back into that swirling, unutterable loneliness of the northland, and he was seeing Conniston again.

Fiercely he caught up the clippings, struck a match, and with a grim smile watched them as they curled up into flame and crumbled into ash. What a lie was life, what a malformed thing was justice, what a monster of iniquity the man-fabricated thing called law!

And again he found himself speaking, as if the dead Englishman himself were repeating the words, "It's devilish queer, old top—and funny!"

CHAPTER 14

A quarter of an hour later, with Mary Josephine at his side, he was walking down the green slope toward the Saskatchewan. In that direction lay the rims of timber, the shimmering valley, and the broad pathways that opened into the plains beyond.

The town was at their backs, and Keith wanted it there. He wanted to keep McDowell, and Shan Tung, and Miriam Kirkstone as far away as possible, until his mind rode more smoothly in the new orbit in which it was still whirling a bit unsteadily. More than all else he wanted to be alone with Mary Josephine, to make sure of her, to convince himself utterly that she was his to go on fighting for. He sensed the nearness and the magnitude of the impending drama. He knew that today he must face Shan Tung, that again he must go under the battery of McDowell's eyes and brain, and that like a fish in treacherous waters he must swim cleverly to avoid the nets that would entangle and destroy him. Today was the day—the stage was set, the curtain about to be lifted, the play ready to be enacted. But before it was the prologue. And the prologue was Mary Josephine's.

At the crest of a dip halfway down the slope they had paused, and in this pause he stood a half-step behind her so that he could look at her for a moment without being observed. She was bareheaded, and it came upon him all at once how wonderful was a woman's hair, how beautiful beyond all other things beautiful and desirable. In twisted, glowing seductiveness it was piled up on Mary Josephine's head, transformed into brown and gold glories by the sun. He wanted to put forth his hand to it, and bury his fingers in it, and feel the thrill and the warmth and the crush of the palpitant life of it against his own flesh. And then, bending a little forward, he saw under her long lashes the sheer joy of life shining in her eyes as she drank in the wonderful panorama that lay below them to the west. Last night's rain had freshened it, the sun glorified it now, and the fragrance of earthly smells that rose up to them from it was the undefiled breath of a thing living and awake. Even to Keith the river had never looked more beautiful, and never had his yearnings gone out to it more strongly than in this moment, to the river and beyond—and to the back of beyond, where the mountains rose up to meet the blue sky and the river itself was born. And he heard Mary Josephine's voice, joyously suppressed, exclaiming softly,

"Oh, Derry!"

His heart was filled with gladness. She, too, was seeing what his eyes saw in that wonderland. And she was feeling it. Her hand, seeking his hand, crept into his palm, and the fingers of it clung to his fingers. He could feel the thrill of the miracle passing through her, the miracle of the open spaces, the miracle of the forests rising billow on billow to the purple mists of the horizon, the miracle of the golden Saskatchewan rolling slowly and peacefully in its slumbering sheen out of that mighty mysteryland that reached to the lap of the setting sun. He spoke to her of that land as she looked, wide-eyed, quick-breathing, her fingers closing still more tightly about his. This was but the beginning of the glory of the west and the north, he told her. Beyond that low horizon, where the tree tops touched the sky were the prairies—not the tiresome monotony which she had seen from the car windows, but the wide, glorious, God-given country of the Northwest with its thousands of lakes and rivers and its tens of thousands of square miles of forests; and beyond those things, still farther, were the foothills, and beyond the foothills the mountains. And in those mountains the river down there had its beginning.

She looked up swiftly, her eyes brimming with the golden flash of the sun. "It is wonderful! And just over there is the town!"

"Yes, and beyond the town are the cities."

"And off there—"

"God's country," said Keith devoutly.

Mary Josephine drew a deep breath. "And people still live in towns and cities!" she exclaimed in wondering credulity. "I've dreamed of 'over here,' Derry, but I never dreamed that. And you've had it for years and years, while I—oh, Derry!"

And again those two words filled his heart with gladness, words of loving reproach, atremble with the mysterious whisper of a great desire. For she was looking into the west. And her eyes and her heart and her soul were in the west, and suddenly Keith saw his way as though lighted by a flaming torch. He came near to forgetting that he was Conniston. He spoke of his dream, his desire, and told her that last night—before she came—he had made up his mind to go. She had come to him just in time. A little later and he would have been gone, buried utterly away from the world in the wonderland of the mountains. And now they would go together. They would go as he had planned to go, quietly, unobtrusively; they would slip away and disappear. There was a reason why no one should know, not even McDowell. It must be their secret. Some day he would tell her why. Her heart thumped excitedly as he went on like a boy planning a wonderful day.

He could see the swifter beat of it in the flush that rose into her face and the joy glowing tremulously in her eyes as she looked at him. They would get ready quietly. They might go tomorrow, the next day, any time. It would be a glorious adventure, just they two, with all the vastness of that mountain paradise ahead of them.

"We'll be pals," he said. "Just you and me, Mary Josephine. We're all that's left."

It was his first experiment, his first reference to the information he had gained in the letters, and swift as a flash Mary Josephine's eyes turned up to him. He nodded, smiling. He understood their quick questioning, and he held her hand closer and began to walk with her down the slope.

"A lot of it came back last night and this morning, a lot of it," he explained. "It's queer what miracles small things can work sometimes, isn't it? Think what a grain of sand can do to a watch! This was one of the small things." He was still smiling as he touched the scar on his forehead. "And you, you were the other miracle. And I'm remembering. It doesn't seem like seven or eight years, but only yesterday, that the grain of sand got mixed up somewhere in the machinery in my head. And I guess there was another reason for my going wrong. You'll understand, when I tell you."

Had he been Conniston it could not have come from him more naturally, more sincerely. He was living the great lie, and yet to him it was no longer a lie. He did not hesitate, as shame and conscience might have made him hesitate. He was fighting that something beautiful might be raised up out of chaos and despair and be made to exist; he was fighting for life in place of death, for happiness in place of grief, for light in place of darkness— fighting to save where others would destroy. Therefore the great lie was not a lie but a thing without venom or hurt, an instrument for happiness and for all the things good and beautiful that went to make happiness. It was his one great weapon. Without it he would fail, and failure meant desolation. So he spoke convincingly, for what he said came straight from the heart though it was born in the shadow of that one master-falsehood. His wonder was that Mary Josephine believed him so utterly that not for an instant was there a questioning doubt in her eyes or on her lips.

He told her how much he "remembered," which was no more and no less than he had learned from the letters and the clippings. The story did not appeal to him as particularly unusual or dramatic. He had passed through too many tragic happenings in the last four years to regard it in that way. It was simply an unfortunate affair beginning in misfortune, and with its necessary whirlwind of hurt and sorrow. The one thing of shame he would not keep out of his mind was that he, Derwent Conniston, must have been a poor type of big brother in those days of nine or ten years ago, even though little Mary Josephine had worshiped him. He was well along in his twenties then. The Connistons of Darlington were his uncle and aunt, and his uncle was a more or less prominent figure in ship-building interests on the Clyde. With these people the three—himself, Mary Josephine, and his brother Egbert—had lived, "farmed out" to a hard-necked, flinty-hearted pair of relatives because of a brother's stipulation and a certain English law. With them they had existed in mutual discontent and dislike. Derwent, when he became old enough, had stepped over the traces. All this Keith had gathered from the letters, but there was a great deal that was missing. Egbert, he gathered, must have been a scapegrace. He was a cripple of some sort and seven or eight years his junior. In the letters Mary Josephine had spoken of him as "poor Egbert," pitying instead of condemning him, though it was Egbert who had brought tragedy and separation upon them. One night Egbert had broken open the Conniston safe and in the darkness had had a fight and a narrow escape from his uncle, who laid the crime upon Derwent. And Derwent, in whom Egbert must have confided, had fled to America that the cripple might be saved, with the promise that some day he would send for Mary Josephine. He was followed by the uncle's threat that if he ever returned to England, he would be jailed. Not long afterward "poor Egbert" was found dead in bed, fearfully contorted. Keith guessed there had been something mentally as well as physically wrong with him.

"—And I was going to send for you," he said, as they came to the level of the valley. "My plans were made, and I was going to send for you, when this came."

He stopped, and in a few tense, breathless moments Mary Josephine read the ninth and last letter he had taken from the Englishman's chest. It was from her uncle. In a dozen lines it stated that she, Mary Josephine, was dead, and it reiterated the threat against Derwent Conniston should he ever dare to return to England.

A choking cry came to her lips. "And that—THAT was it?"

"Yes, that—and the hurt in my head," he said, remembering the part he must play. "They came at about the same time, and the two of them must have put the grain of sand in my brain."

It was hard to lie now, looking straight into her face that had gone suddenly white, and with her wonderful eyes burning deep into his soul.

She did not seem, for an instant, to hear his voice or sense his words. "I understand now," she was saying, the letter crumpling in her fingers. "I was sick for almost a year, Derry. They thought I was going to die. He must have written it then, and they destroyed my letters to you, and when I was better they told me you were dead, and then I didn't write any more. And I wanted to die. And then, almost a year ago, Colonel Reppington came to me, and his dear old voice was so excited that it trembled, and he told me that he believed you were alive. A friend of his had just returned from British Columbia, and this friend told him that three years before, while on a grizzly shooting trip, he had met a man named Conniston, an Englishman. We wrote a hundred letters up there and found the man, Jack Otto, who was in the mountains with you, and then I knew you were alive. But we couldn't find you after that, and so I came—"

He would have wagered that she was going to cry, but she fought the tears back, smiling.

"And—and I've found you!" she finished triumphantly.

She snuggled close to him, and he slipped an arm about her waist, and they walked on. She told him about her arrival in Halifax, how Colonel Reppington had given her letters to nice people in Montreal and Winnipeg, and how it happened one day that she found his name in one of the Mounted Police blue books, and after that came on as fast as she could to surprise him at Prince Albert. When she came to that point, Keith pointed once more into the west and said:

"And there is our new world. Let us forget the old. Shall we, Mary Josephine?"

"Yes," she whispered, and her hand sought his again and crept into it, warm and confident.

CHAPTER 15

They went on through the golden morning, the earth damp under their feet, the air filled with its sweet incense, on past scattered clumps of balsams and cedars until they came to the river and looked down on its yellow sand-bars glistening in the sun. The town was hidden. They heard no sound from it. And looking up the great Saskatchewan, the river of mystery, of romance, of glamour, they saw before them, where the spruce walls seemed to meet, the wide-open door through which they might pass into the western land beyond. Keith pointed it out. And he pointed out the yellow bars, the glistening shores of sand, and told her how even as far as this, a thousand miles by river—those sands brought gold with them from the mountains, the gold whose treasure-house no man had ever found, and which must be hidden up there somewhere near the river's end. His dream, like Duggan's, had been to find it. Now they would search for it together.

Slowly he was picking his way so that at last they came to the bit of cleared timber in which was his old home. His heart choked him as they drew near. There was an uncomfortable tightness in his breath. The timber was no longer "clear." In four years younger generations of life had sprung up among the trees, and the place was jungle-ridden. They were within a few yards of the house before Mary Josephine saw it, and then she stopped suddenly with a little gasp. For this that she faced was not desertion, was not mere neglect. It was tragedy. She saw in an instant that there was no life in this place, and yet it stood as if tenanted. It was a log chateau with a great, red chimney rising at one end curtains and shades still hung at the windows. There were three chairs on the broad veranda that looked riverward. But two of the windows were broken, and the chairs were falling into ruin. There was no life. They were facing only the ghosts of life.

A swift glance into Keith's face told her this was so. His lips were set tight. There was a strange look in his face. Hand in hand they had come up, and her fingers pressed his tighter now.

"What is it?" she asked.

"It is John Keith's home as he left it four years ago," he replied.

The suspicious break in his voice drew her eyes from the chateau to his own again. She could see him fighting. There was a twitching in his throat. His hand was gripping hers until it hurt.

"John Keith?" she whispered softly.

"Yes, John Keith."

She inclined her head so that it rested lightly and affectionately against his arm.

"You must have thought a great deal of him, Derry."

"Yes."

He freed her hand, and his fists clenched convulsively. She could feel the cording of the muscles in his arm, his face was white, and in his eyes was a fixed stare that startled her. He fumbled in a pocket and drew out a key.

"I promised, when he died, that I would go in and take a last look for him," he said. "He loved this place. Do you want to go with me?"

She drew a deep breath. "Yes."

The key opened the door that entered on the veranda. As it swung back, grating on its rusty hinges, they found themselves facing the chill of a cold and lifeless air. Keith stepped inside. A glance told him that nothing was changed—everything was there in that room with the big fireplace, even as he had left it the night he set out to force justice from Judge Kirkstone. One thing startled him. On the dust-covered table was a bowl and a spoon. He remembered vividly how he had eaten his supper that night of bread and milk. It was the littleness of the thing, the simplicity of it, that shocked him. The bowl and spoon were still there after four years. He did not reflect that they were as imperishable as all the other things about; the miracle was that they were there on the table, as though he had used them only yesterday. The most trivial things in the room struck him deepest, and he found himself fighting hard, for a moment, to keep his nerve.

"He told me about the bowl and the spoon, John Keith did," he said, nodding toward them. "He told me just what I'd find here, even to that. You see, he loved the place greatly and everything that was in it. It was impossible for him to forget even the bowl and the spoon and where he had left them."

It was easier after that. The old home was whispering back its memories to him, and he told them to Mary Josephine as they went slowly from room to room, until John Keith was living there before her again, the John Keith whom Derwent Conniston had run to his death. It was this thing that gripped her, and at last what was in her mind found voice.

"It wasn't YOU who made him die, was it, Derry? It wasn't you?"

"No. It was the law. He died, as I told you, of a frosted lung. At the last I would have shared my life with him had it been possible. McDowell must never know that. You must never speak of John Keith before him."

"I—I understand, Derry."

"And he must not know that we came here. To him John Keith was a murderer whom it was his duty to hang."

She was looking at him strangely. Never had he seen her look at him in that way.

"Derry," she whispered.

"Yes?"

"Derry, IS JOHN KEITH ALIVE?"

He started. The shock of the question was in his face. He caught himself, but it was too late. And in an instant her hand was at his mouth, and she was whispering eagerly, almost fiercely:

"No, no, no—don't answer me, Derry! DON'T ANSWER ME! I know, and I understand, and I'm glad, glad, GLAD! He's alive, and it was you who let him live, the big, glorious brother I'm proud of! And everyone else thinks he's dead. But don't answer me, Derry, don't answer me!"

She was trembling against him. His arms closed about her, and he held her nearer to his heart, and longer, than he had ever held her before. He kissed her hair many times, and her lips once, and up about his neck her arms twined softly, and a great brightness was in her eyes.

"I understand," she whispered again. "I understand."

"And I—I must answer you," he said. "I must answer you, because I love you, and because you must know. Yes, John Keith is alive!"

CHAPTER 16

An hour later, alone and heading for the inspector's office, Keith felt in battle trim. His head was fairly singing with the success of the morning. Since the opening of Conniston's chest many things had happened, and he was no longer facing a blank wall of mystery. His chief cause of exhilaration was Mary Josephine. She wanted to go away with him. She wanted to go with him anywhere, everywhere, as long as they were together. When she had learned that his term of enlistment was about to expire and that if he remained in the Service he would be away from her a great deal, she had pleaded with him not to reenlist. She did not question him when he told her that it might be necessary to go away very suddenly, without letting another soul know of their movements, not even Wallie. Intuitively she guessed that the reason had something to do with John Keith, for he had let the fear grow in her that McDowell might discover he had been a traitor to the Service, in which event the Law itself would take him away from her for a considerable number of years. And with that fear she was more than ever eager for the adventure, and planned with him for its consummation.

Another thing cheered Keith. He was no longer the absolute liar of yesterday, for by a fortunate chance he had been able to tell her that John Keith was alive. This most important of all truths he had confided to her, and the confession had roused in her a comradeship that had proclaimed itself ready to fight for him or run away with him. Not for an instant had she regretted the action he had taken in giving Keith his freedom. He was peculiarly happy because of that. She was glad John Keith was alive.

And now that she knew the story of the old home down in the clump of timber and of the man who had lived there, she was anxious to meet Miriam Kirkstone, daughter of the man he had killed. Keith had promised her they would go up that afternoon. Within himself he knew that he was not sure of keeping the promise. There was much to do in the next few hours, and much might happen. In fact there was but little speculation about it. This was the big day. Just what it held for him he could not be sure until he saw Shan Tung. Any instant might see him put to the final test.

Cruze was pacing slowly up and down the hall when Keith entered the building in which McDowell had his offices. The young secretary's face bore a perplexed and rather anxious expression. His hands were buried deep in his trousers pockets, and he was puffing a cigarette. At Keith's appearance he brightened up a bit.

"Don't know what to make of the governor this morning, by Jove I don't!" he explained, nodding toward the closed doors. "I've got instructions to let no one near him except you. You may go in."

"What seems to be the matter?" Keith felt out cautiously.

Cruze shrugged his thin shoulders, nipped the ash from his cigarette, and with a grimace said, "Shan Tung."

"Shan Tung?" Keith spoke the name in a sibilant whisper. Every nerve in him had jumped, and for an instant he thought he had betrayed himself. Shan Tung had been there early. And now McDowell was waiting for him and had given instructions that no other should be admitted. If the Chinaman had exposed him, why hadn't McDowell sent officers up to the Shack? That was the first question that jumped into his head. The answer came as quickly—McDowell had not sent officers because, hating Shan Tung, he had not believed his story. But he was waiting there to investigate. A chill crept over Keith.

Cruze was looking at him intently.

"There's something to this Shan Tung business," he said. "It's even getting on the old man's nerves. And he's very anxious to see you, Mr. Conniston. I've called you up half a dozen times in the last hour."

He nipped away his cigarette, turned alertly, and moved toward the inspector's door. Keith wanted to call him back, to leap upon him, if necessary, and drag him away from that deadly door. But he neither moved nor spoke until it was too late. The door opened, he heard Cruze announce his presence, and it seemed to him the words were scarcely out of the secretary's mouth when McDowell himself stood in the door.

"Come in, Conniston," he said quietly. "Come in."

It was not McDowell's voice. It was restrained, terrible. It was the voice of a man speaking softly to cover a terrific fire raging within. Keith felt himself doomed. Even as he entered, his mind was swiftly gathering itself for the last play, the play he had set for himself if the crisis came. He would cover McDowell, bind and gag him even as Cruze sauntered in the hall, escape through a window, and with Mary Josephine bury himself in the forests before pursuit could overtake them. Therefore his amazement was unbounded when McDowell, closing the door, seized his hand in a grip that made him wince, and shook it with unfeigned gladness and relief.

"I'm not condemning you, of course," he said. "It was rather beastly of me to annoy your sister before you were up this morning. She flatly refused to rouse you, and by George, the way she said it made me turn the business of getting into touch with you over to Cruze. Sit down, Conniston. I'm going to explode a mine under you."

He flung himself into his swivel chair and twisted one of his fierce mustaches, while his eyes blazed at Keith. Keith waited. He saw the other was like an animal ready to spring and anxious to spring, the one evident stricture on his desire being that there was nothing to spring at unless it was himself.

"What happened last night?" he asked.

Keith's mind was already working swiftly. McDowell's question gave him the opportunity of making the first play against Shan Tung.

"Enough to convince me that I am going to see Shan Tung today," he said.

He noticed the slow clenching and unclenching of McDowell's fingers about the arms of his chair.

"Then—I was right?"

"I have every reason to believe you were—up to a certain point. I shall know positively when I have talked with Shan Tung."

He smiled grimly. McDowell's eyes were no harder than his own. The iron man drew a deep breath and relaxed a bit in his chair.

"If anything should happen," he said, looking away from Keith, as though the speech were merely casual, "if he attacks you—"

"It might be necessary to kill him in self-defense," finished Keith.

McDowell made no sign to show that he had heard, yet Keith thrilled with the conviction that he had struck home. He went on telling briefly what had happened at Miriam Kirkstone's house the preceding night. McDowell's face was purple when he described the evidences of Shan Tung's presence at the house on the hill, but with a mighty effort he restrained his passion.

"That's it, that's it," he exclaimed, choking back his wrath. "I knew he was there! And this morning both of them lie about it—both of them, do you understand! She lied, looking me straight in the eyes. And he lied, and for the first time in his life he laughed at me, curse me if he didn't! It was like the gurgle of oil. I didn't know a human could laugh that way. And on top of that he told me something that I WON'T believe, so help me God, I won't!"

He jumped to his feet and began pacing back and forth, his hands clenched behind him. Suddenly he whirled on Keith.

"Why in heaven's name didn't you bring Keith back with you, or, if not Keith, at least a written confession, signed by him?" he demanded.

This was a blow from behind for Keith. "What—what has Keith got to do with this?" he stumbled.

"More than I dare tell you, Conniston. But WHY didn't you bring back a signed confession from him? A dying man is usually willing to make that."

"If he is guilty, yes," agreed Keith. "But this man was a different sort. If he killed Judge Kirkstone, he had no regret. He did not consider himself a criminal. He felt that he had dealt out justice in his own way, and therefore, even when he was dying, he would not sign anything or state anything definitely."

McDowell subsided into his chair.

"And the curse of it is I haven't a thing on Shan Tung," he gritted. "Not a thing. Miriam Kirkstone is her own mistress, and in the eyes of the law he is as innocent of crime as I am. If she is voluntarily giving herself as a victim to this devil, it is her own business—legally, you understand. Morally—"

He stopped, his savagely gleaming eyes boring Keith to the marrow.

"He hates you as a snake hates fire-water. It is possible, if he thought the opportunity had come to him—"

Again he paused, cryptic, waiting for the other to gather the thing he had not spoken. Keith, simulating two of Conniston's tricks at the same time, shrugged a shoulder and twisted a mustache as he rose to his feet. He smiled coolly down at the iron man. For once he gave a passable imitation of the Englishman.

"And he's going to have the opportunity today," he said understandingly. "I think, old chap, I'd better be going. I'm rather anxious to see Shan Tung before dinner."

McDowell followed him to the door.

His face had undergone a change. There was a tense expectancy, almost an eagerness there. Again he gripped Keith's hand, and before the door opened he said,

"If trouble comes between you let it be in the open, Conniston—in the open and not on Shan Tung's premises."

Keith went out, his pulse quickening to the significance of the iron man's words, and wondering what the "mine" was that McDowell had promised to explode, but which he had not.

CHAPTER 17

Keith lost no time in heading for Shan Tung's. He was like a man playing chess, and the moves were becoming so swift and so intricate that his mind had no rest. Each hour brought forth its fresh necessities and its new alternatives. It was McDowell who had given him his last cue, perhaps the surest and safest method of all for winning his game. The iron man, that disciple of the Law who was merciless in his demand of an eye for an eye and a tooth for a tooth, had let him understand that the world would be better off without Shan Tung. This man, who never in his life had found an excuse for the killer, now maneuvered subtly the suggestion for a killing.

Keith was both shocked and amazed. "If anything happens, let it be in the open and not on Shan Tung's premises," he had warned him. That implied in McDowell's mind a cool and calculating premeditation, the assumption that if Shan Tung was killed it would be in self-defense. And Keith's blood leaped to the thrill of it. He had not only found the depths of McDowell's personal interest in Miriam Kirkstone, but a last weapon had been placed in his hands, a weapon which he could use this day if it became necessary. Cornered, with no other hope of saving himself, he could as a last resort kill Shan Tung—and McDowell would stand behind him!

He went directly to Shan Tung's cafe and sauntered in. There were large changes in it since four years ago. The moment he passed through its screened vestibule, he felt its oriental exclusiveness, the sleek and mysterious quietness of it. One might have found such a place catering to the elite of a big city. It spoke sumptuously of a large expenditure of money, yet there was nothing bizarre or irritating to the senses. Its heavily-carved tables were almost oppressive in their solidity. Linen and silver, like Shan Tung himself, were immaculate. Magnificently embroidered screens were so cleverly arranged that one saw not all of the place at once, but caught vistas of it. The few voices that Keith heard in this pre-lunch hour were subdued, and the speakers were concealed by screens. Two orientals, as immaculate as the silver and linen, were moving about with the silence of velvet-padded lynxes. A third, far in the rear, stood motionless as one of the carven tables, smoking a cigarette and watchful as a ferret. This was Li King, Shan Tung's right-hand man.

Keith approached him. When he was near enough, Li King gave the slightest inclination to his head and took the cigarette from his mouth.

Without movement or speech he registered the question, "What do you want?"

Keith knew this to be a bit of oriental guile. In his mind there was no doubt that Li King had been fully instructed by his master and that he had been expecting him, even watching for him. Convinced of this, he gave him one of Conniston's cards and said,

"Take this to Shan Tung. He is expecting me."

Li King looked at the card, studied it for a moment with apparent stupidity, and shook his head. "Shan Tung no home. Gone away."

That was all. Where he had gone or when he would return Keith could not discover from Li King. Of all other matters except that he had gone away the manager of Shan Tung's affairs was ignorant. Keith felt like taking the yellow-skinned hypocrite by the throat and choking something out of him, but he realized that Li King was studying and watching him, and that he would report to Shan Tung every expression that had passed over his face. So he looked at his watch, bought a cigar at the glass case near the cash register, and departed with a cheerful nod, saying that he would call again.

Ten minutes later he determined on a bold stroke. There was no time for indecision or compromise. He must find Shan Tung and find him quickly. And he believed that Miriam Kirkstone could give him a pretty good tip as to his whereabouts. He steeled himself to the demand he was about to make as he strode up to the house on the hill. He was disappointed again. Miss Kirkstone was not at home. If she was, she did not answer to his knocking and bell ringing.

He went to the depot. No one he questioned had seen Shan Tung at the west-bound train, the only train that had gone out that morning, and the agent emphatically disclaimed selling him a ticket. Therefore he had not gone far. Suspicion leaped red in Keith's brain. His imagination pictured Shan Tung at that moment with Miriam Kirkstone, and at the thought his disgust went out against them both. In this humor he returned to McDowell's office. He stood before his chief, leaning toward him over the desk table. This time he was the inquisitor.

"Plainly speaking, this liaison is their business," he declared. "Because he is yellow and she is white doesn't make it ours. I've just had a hunch. And I believe in following hunches, especially when one hits you good and hard, and this one has given me a jolt that means something. Where is that big fat brother of hers?"

McDowell hesitated. "It isn't a liaison," he temporized. "It's one-sided—a crime against—"

"WHERE IS THAT BIG FAT BROTHER?" With each word Keith emphasized his demand with a thud of his fist on the table. "WHERE IS HE?"

McDowell was deeply perturbed. Keith could see it and waited.

After a moment of silence the iron man rose from the swivel chair, walked to the window, gazed out for another moment, and walked back again, twisting one of his big gray mustaches in a way that betrayed the stress of his emotion. "Confound it, Conniston, you've got a mind for seeking out the trivialities, and little things are sometimes the most embarrassing."

"And sometimes most important," added Keith. "For instance, it strikes me as mighty important that we should know where Peter Kirkstone is and why he is not here fighting for his sister's salvation. Where is he?"

"I don't know. He disappeared from town a month ago. Miriam says he is somewhere in British Columbia looking over some old mining properties. She doesn't know just where."

"And you believe her?"

The eyes of the two men met. There was no longer excuse for equivocation. Both understood.

McDowell smiled in recognition of the fact. "No. I think, Conniston, that she is the most wonderful little liar that lives. And the beautiful part of it is, she is lying for a purpose. Imagine Peter Kirkstone, who isn't worth the powder to blow him to Hades, interested in old mines or anything else that promises industry or production! And the most inconceivable thing about the whole mess is that Miriam worships that fat and worthless pig of a brother. I've tried to find him in British Columbia. Failed, of course. Another proof that this affair between Miriam and Shan Tung isn't a voluntary liaison on her part. She's lying. She's walking on a pavement of lies. If she told the truth—"

"There are some truths which one cannot tell about oneself," interrupted Keith. "They must be discovered or buried. And I'm going deeper into this prospecting and undertaking business this afternoon. I've got another hunch. I think I'll have something interesting to report before night."

Ten minutes later, on his way to the Shack, he was discussing with himself the modus operandi of that "hunch." It had come to him in an instant, a flash of inspiration. That afternoon he would see Miriam Kirkstone and question her about Peter. Then he would return to

McDowell, lay stress on the importance of the brother, tell him that he had a clew which he wanted to follow, and suggest finally a swift trip to British Columbia. He would take Mary Josephine, lie low until his term of service expired, and then report by letter to McDowell that he had failed and that he had made up his mind not to reenlist but to try his fortunes with Mary Josephine in Australia. Before McDowell received that letter, they could be on their way into the mountains. The "hunch" offered an opportunity for a clean getaway, and in his jubilation Miriam Kirkstone and her affairs were important only as a means to an end. He was John Keith now, fighting for John Keith's life—and Derwent Conniston's sister.

Mary Josephine herself put the first shot into the fabric of his plans. She must have been watching for him, for when halfway up the slope he saw her coming to meet him. She scolded him for being away from her, as he had expected her to do. Then she pulled his arm about her slim little waist and held the hand thus engaged in both her own as they walked up the winding path. He noticed the little wrinkles in her adorable forehead.

"Derry, is it the right thing for young ladies to call on their gentlemen friends over here?" she asked suddenly.

"Why—er—that depends, Mary Josephine. You mean—"

"Yes, I do, Derwent Conniston! She's pretty, and I don't blame you, but I can't help feeling that I don't like it!"

His arm tightened about her until she gasped. The fragile softness of her waist was a joy to him.

"Derry!" she remonstrated. "If you do that again, I'll break!"

"I couldn't help it," he pleaded. "I couldn't, dear. The way you said it just made my arm close up tight. I'm glad you didn't like it. I can love only one at a time, and I'm loving you, and I'm going on loving you all my life."

"I wasn't jealous," she protested, blushing. "But she called twice on the telephone and then came up. And she's pretty."

"I suppose you mean Miss Kirkstone?"

"Yes. She was frightfully anxious to see you, Derry."

"And what did you think of her, dear?"

She cast a swift look up into his face.

"Why, I like her. She's sweet and pretty, and I fell in love with her hair. But something was troubling her this morning. I'm quite sure of it, though she tried to keep it back."

"She was nervous, you mean, and pale, with sometimes a frightened look in her eyes. Was that it?"

"You seem to know, Derry. I think it was all that."

He nodded. He saw his horizon aglow with the smile of fortune. Everything was coming propitiously for him, even this unexpected visit of Miriam Kirkstone. He did not trouble himself to speculate as to the object of her visit, for he was grappling now with his own opportunity, his chance to get away, to win out for himself in one last master-stroke, and his mind was concentrated in that direction. The time was ripe to tell these things to Mary Josephine. She must be prepared.

On the flat table of the hill where Brady had built his bungalow were scattered clumps of golden birch, and in the shelter of one of the nearer clumps was a bench, to which Keith drew Mary Josephine. Thereafter for many minutes he spoke his plans. Mary Josephine's cheeks grew flushed. Her eyes shone with excitement and eagerness. She thrilled to the story he told her of what they would do in those wonderful mountains of gold and mystery, just they two alone. He made her understand even more definitely that his safety and their mutual happiness depended upon the secrecy of their final project, that in a way they were conspirators and must act as such. They might start for the west tonight or tomorrow, and she must get ready.

There he should have stopped. But with Mary Josephine's warm little hand clinging to his and her beautiful eyes shining at him like liquid stars, he felt within him an overwhelming faith and desire, and he went on, making a clean breast of the situation that was giving them the opportunity to get away. He felt no prick of conscience at thought of Miriam Kirkstone's affairs. Her destiny must be, as he had told McDowell, largely a matter of her own choosing. Besides, she had McDowell to fight for her. And the big fat brother, too. So without fear of its effect he told Mary Josephine of the mysterious liaison between Miriam Kirkstone and Shan Tung, of McDowell's suspicions, of his own beliefs, and how it was all working out for their own good.

Not until then did he begin to see the changing lights in her eyes. Not until he had finished did he notice that most of that vivid flush of joy had gone from her face and that she was looking at him in a strained, tense way. He felt then the reaction. She was not looking at the thing as he was looking at it. He had offered to her another woman's tragedy as THEIR opportunity, and her own woman's heart had responded in the way that has been woman's since the dawn of life. A sense of shame which he fought and tried to crush took possession of him. He was right. He must be right, for it was his life that was hanging in the balance. Yet Mary Josephine could not know that.

94

Her fingers had tightened about his, and she was looking away from him. He saw now that the color had almost gone from her face. There was the flash of a new fire in her yes.

"And THAT was why she was nervous and pale, with sometimes a frightened look in her eyes," she spoke softly, repeating his words. "It was because of this Chinese monster, Shan Tung—because he has some sort of power over her, you say—because—"

She snatched her hand from his with a suddenness that startled him. Her eyes, so beautiful and soft a few minutes before, scintillated fire. "Derry, if you don't fix this heathen devil—I WILL!"

She stood up before him, breathing quickly, and he beheld in her not the soft, slim-waisted little goddess of half an hour ago, but the fiercest fighter of all the fighting ages, a woman roused. And no longer fear, but a glory swept over him. She was Conniston's sister, AND SHE WAS CONNISTON. Even as he saw his plans falling about him, he opened his arms and held them out to her, and with the swiftness of love she ran into them, putting her hands to his face while he held her close and kissed her lips.

"You bet we'll fix that heathen devil before we go," he said. "You bet we will—SWEETHEART!"

CHAPTER 18

Wallie, suffering the outrage of one who sees his dinner growing cold, found Keith and Mary Josephine in the edge of the golden birch and implored them to come and eat. It was a marvel of a dinner. Over Mary Josephine's coffee and Keith's cigar they discussed their final plans. Keith made the big promise that he would "fix Shan Tung" in a hurry, perhaps that very afternoon. In the glow of Mary Josephine's proud eyes he felt no task too large for him, and he was eager to be at it. But when his cigar was half done, Mary Josephine came around and perched herself on the arm of his chair, and began running her fingers through his hair. All desire to go after Shan Tung left him. He would have remained there forever. Twice she bent down and touched his forehead lightly with her lips. Again his arm was round her soft little waist, and his heart was pumping like a thing overworked. It was Mary Josephine, finally, who sent him on his mission, but not before she stood on tiptoe, her hands on his shoulders, giving him her mouth to kiss.

An army at his back could not have strengthened Keith with a vaster determination than that kiss. There would be no more quibbling. His mind was made up definitely on the point. And his first move was to head straight for the Kirkstone house on the hill.

He did not get as far as the door this time. He caught a vision of Miriam Kirkstone in the shrubbery, bareheaded, her hair glowing radiantly in the sun. It occurred to him suddenly that it was her hair that roused the venom in him when he thought of her as the property of Shan Tung. If it had been black or even brown, the thought might not have emphasized itself so unpleasantly in his mind. But that vivid gold cried out against the crime, even against the girl herself. She saw him almost in the instant his eyes fell upon her, and came forward quickly to meet him. There was an eagerness in her face that told him his coming relieved her of a terrific suspense.

"I'm sorry I wasn't at the Shack when you came, Miss Kirkstone," he said, taking for a moment the hand she offered him. "I fancy you were up there to see me about Shan Tung."

He sent the shot bluntly, straight home. In the tone of his voice there was no apology. He saw her grow cold, her eyes fixed on him staringly, as though she not only heard his words but saw what was in his mind.

"Wasn't that it, Miss Kirkstone?"

She nodded affirmatively, but her lips did not move.

"Shan Tung," he repeated. "Miss Kirkstone, what is the trouble? Why don't you confide in someone, in McDowell, in me, in—"

He was going to say "your brother," but the suddenness with which she caught his arm cut the words short.

"Shan Tung has been to see him—McDowell?" she questioned excitedly. "He has been there today? And he told him—" She stopped, breathing quickly, her fingers tightening on his arm.

"I don't know what passed between them," said Keith. "But McDowell was tremendously worked up about you. So am I. We might as well be frank, Miss Kirkstone. There's something rotten in Denmark when two people like you and Shan Tung mix up. And you are mixed; you can't deny it. You have been to see Shan Tung late at night. He was in the house with you the first night I saw you. More than that—HE IS IN YOUR HOUSE NOW!"

She shrank back as if he had struck at her. "No, no, no," she cried. "He isn't there. I tell you, he isn't!"

"How am I to believe you?" demanded Keith. "You have not told the truth to McDowell. You are fighting to cover up the truth. And we know it is because of Shan Tung. WHY? I am here to fight for you, to help you. And McDowell, too. That is why we must know. Miss Kirkstone, do you love the Chinaman?"

He knew the words were an insult. He had guessed their effect. As if struck there suddenly by a painter's brush, two vivid spots appeared in the girl's pale cheeks. She shrank back from him another step. Her eyes blazed. Slowly, without turning their flame from his face, she pointed to the edge of the shrubbery a few feet from where they were standing. He looked. Twisted and partly coiled on the mold, where it had been clubbed to death, was a little green grass snake.

"I hate him—like that!" she said.

His eyes came back to her. "Then for some reason known only to you and Shan Tung you have sold or are intending to sell yourself to him!"

It was not a question. It was an accusation. He saw the flush of anger fading out of her cheeks. Her body relaxed, her head dropped, and slowly she nodded in confirmation.

"Yes, I am going to sell myself to him."

The astounding confession held him mute for a space. In the interval it was the girl who became self-possessed. What she said next amazed him still more.

"I have confessed so much because I am positive that you will not betray me. And I went up to the Shack to find you, because I want you to help me find a story to tell McDowell. You said you would help me. Will you?"

He still did not speak, and she went on.

"I am accepting that promise as granted, too. McDowell mistrusts, but he must not know. You must help me there. You must help me for two or three weeks, At the end of that time something may happen. He must be made to have faith in me again. Do you understand?"

"Partly," said Keith. "You ask me to do this blindly, without knowing why I am doing it, without any explanation whatever on your part except that for some unknown and mysterious price you are going to sell yourself to Shan Tung. You want me to cover and abet this monstrous deal by hoodwinking the man whose suspicions threaten its consummation. If there was not in my own mind a suspicion that you are insane, I should say your proposition is as ludicrous as it is impossible. Having that suspicion, it is a bit tragic. Also it is impossible. It is necessary for you first to tell me why you are going to sell yourself to Shan Tung."

Her face was coldly white and calm again. But her hands trembled. He saw her try to hide them, and pitied her.

"Then I won't trouble you any more, for that, too, is impossible," she said. "May I trust you to keep in confidence what I have told you? Perhaps I have had too much faith in you for a reason which has no reason, because you were with John Keith. John Keith was the one other man who might have helped me."

"And why John Keith? How could he have helped you?"

She shook her head. "If I told you that, I should be answering the question which is impossible."

He saw himself facing a checkmate. To plead, to argue with her, he knew would profit him nothing. A new thought came to him, swift and imperative. The end would justify the means. He clenched his hands. He forced into his face a look that was black and vengeful. And he turned it on her.

"Listen to me," he cried. "You are playing a game, and so am I. Possibly we are selfish, both of us, looking each to his own interests with no thought of the other. Will you help me, if I help you?"

Again he pitied her as he saw with what eager swiftness she caught at his bait.

"Yes," she nodded, catching her breath. "Yes, I will help you."

His face grew blacker. He raised his clenched hands so she could see them, and advanced a step toward her.

"Then tell me this—would you care if something happened to Shan Tung? Would you care if he died, if he was killed, if—"

Her breath was coming faster and faster. Again the red spots blazed in her cheeks.

"WOULD YOU CARE?" he demanded.

"No—no—I wouldn't care. He deserves to die."

"Then tell me where Shan Tung is. For my game is with him. And I believe it is a bigger game than your game, for it is a game of life and death. That is why I am interested in your affair. It is because I am selfish, because I have my own score to settle, and because you can help me. I shall ask you no more questions about yourself. And I shall keep your secret and help you with McDowell if you will keep mine and help me. First, where is Shan Tung?"

She hesitated for barely an instant. "He has gone out of town. He will be away for ten days."

"But he bought no ticket; no one saw him leave by train."

"No, he walked up the river. An auto was waiting for him. He will pass through tonight on the eastbound train on his way to Winnipeg."

"Will you tell me why he is going to Winnipeg?"

"No, I cannot."

He shrugged his shoulders. "It is scarcely necessary to ask. I can guess. It is to see your brother."

Again he knew he had struck home.

And yet she said, "No, it is not to see my brother."

He held out his hand to her. "Miss Kirkstone, I am going to keep my promise. I am going to help you with McDowell. Of course I demand my price. Will you swear on your word of honor to let me know the moment Shan Tung returns?"

"I will let you know."

Their hands clasped. Looking into her eyes, Keith saw what told him his was not the greatest cross to bear. Miriam Kirkstone also was fighting for her life, and as he turned to leave her, he said:

"While there is life there is hope. In settling my score with Shan Tung I believe that I shall also settle yours. It is a strong hunch, Miss Kirkstone, and it's holding me tight. Ten days, Shan Tung, and then—"

He left her, smiling. Miriam Kirkstone watched him go, her slim hands clutched at her breast, her eyes aglow with a new thought, a new hope; and

99

as he heard the gate slam behind him, a sobbing cry rose in her throat, and she reached out her hands as if to call him back, for something was telling her that through this man lay the way to her salvation.

And her lips were moaning softly, "Ten days—ten days—and then—what?"

CHAPTER 19

In those ten days all the wonders of June came up out of the south. Life pulsed with a new and vibrant force. The crimson fire-flowers, first of wild blooms to come after snow and frost, splashed the green spaces with red. The forests took on new colors, the blue of the sky grew nearer, and in men's veins the blood ran with new vigor and anticipations. To Keith they were all this and more. Four years along the rim of the Arctic had made it possible for him to drink to the full the glory of early summer along the Saskatchewan. And to Mary Josephine it was all new. Never had she seen a summer like this that was dawning, that most wonderful of all the summers in the world, which comes in June along the southern edge of the Northland.

Keith had played his promised part. It was not difficult for him to wipe away the worst of McDowell's suspicions regarding Miss Kirkstone, for McDowell was eager to believe. When Keith told him that Miriam was on the verge of a nervous breakdown simply because of certain trouble into which Shan Tung had inveigled her brother, and that everything would be straightened out the moment Shan Tung returned from Winnipeg, the iron man seized his hands in a sudden burst of relief and gratitude.

"But why didn't she confide in me, Conniston?" he complained. "Why didn't she confide in me?" The anxiety in his voice, its note of disappointment, were almost boyish.

Keith was prepared. "Because—"

He hesitated, as if projecting the thing in his mind. "McDowell, I'm in a delicate position. You must understand without forcing me to say too much. You are the last man in the world Miss Kirkstone wants to know about her trouble until she has triumphed, and it is over. Delicacy, perhaps; a woman's desire to keep something she is ashamed of from the one man she looks up to above all other men—to keep it away from him until she has cleared herself so that there is no suspicion. McDowell, if I were you, I'd be proud of her for that."

McDowell turned away, and for a space Keith saw the muscles in the back of his neck twitching.

"Derwent, maybe you've guessed, maybe you understand," he said after a moment with his face still turned to the window. "Of course she will never know. I'm too Old, old enough to be her father. But I've got the right to watch over her, and if any man ever injures her—"

His fists grew knotted, and softly Keith said behind him:

"You'd possibly do what John Keith did to the man who wronged his father. And because the Law is not always omniscient, it is also possible that Shan Tung may have to answer in some such way. Until then, until she comes to you of her own free will and with gladness in her eyes tells you her own secret and why she kept it from you—until she does that, I say, it is your part to treat her as if you had seen nothing, guessed nothing, suspected nothing. Do that, McDowell, and leave the rest to me."

He went out, leaving the iron man still with his face to the window.

With Mary Josephine there was no subterfuge. His mind was still centered in his own happiness. He could not wipe out of his brain the conviction that if he waited for Shan Tung he was waiting just so long under the sword of Damocles, with a hair between him and doom. He hoped that Miriam Kirkstone's refusal to confide in him and her reluctance to furnish him with the smallest facts in the matter would turn Mary Josephine's sympathy into a feeling of indifference if not of actual resentment. He was disappointed. Mary Josephine insisted on having Miss Kirkstone over for dinner the next day, and from that hour something grew between the two girls which Keith knew he was powerless to overcome. Thereafter he bowed his head to fate. He must wait for Shan Tung.

"If it wasn't for your promise not to fall in love, I'd be afraid," Mary Josephine confided to him that night, perched on the arm of his big chair. "At times I was afraid today, Derry. She's lovely. And you like pretty hair—and hers—is wonderful!"

"I don't remember," said Keith quietly, "that I promised you I wouldn't fall in love. I'm desperately in love, and with you, Mary Josephine. And as for Miss Kirkstone's lovely hair—I wouldn't trade one of yours for all she has on her head."

At that, with a riotous little laugh of joy, Mary Josephine swiftly unbound her hair and let it smother about his face and shoulders. "Sometimes I have a terribly funny thought, Derry," she whispered. "If we hadn't always been sweethearts, back there at home, and if you hadn't always liked my hair, and kissed me, and told me I was pretty, I'd almost think you weren't my brother!"

Keith laughed and was glad that her hair covered his face. During those wonderful first days of the summer they were inseparable, except when matters of business took Keith away. During these times he prepared for eventualities. The Keith properties in Prince Albert, he estimated, were worth at least a hundred thousand dollars, and he learned from McDowell that they would soon go through a process of law before being turned over to his fortunate inheritors. Before that time, however, he knew that his own fate would be sealed one way or the other, and now that he had Mary Josephine to look after, he made a will, leaving everything to her, and signing himself John Keith. This will he carried in an envelope pinned inside his shirt. As Derwent Conniston he collected one thousand two hundred and sixty dollars for three and a half years back wage in the Service. Two hundred and sixty of this he kept in his own pocket. The remaining thousand he counted out in new hundred-dollar bills under Mary Josephine's eyes, sealed the bills in another envelope, and gave the envelope to her.

"It's safer with you than with me," he excused himself. "Fasten it inside your dress. It's our grub-stake into the mountains."

Mary Josephine accepted the treasure with the repressed delight of one upon whose fair shoulders had been placed a tremendous responsibility.

There were days of both joy and pain for Keith. For even in the fullest hours of his happiness there was a thing eating at his heart, a thing that was eating deeper and deeper until at times it was like a destroying flame within him. One night he dreamed; he dreamed that Conniston came to his bedside and wakened him, and that after wakening him he taunted him in ghoulish glee and told him that in bequeathing him a sister he had given unto him forever and forever the curse of the daughters of Achelous. And Keith, waking in the dark hour of night, knew in his despair that it was so. For all time, even though he won this fight he was fighting, Mary Josephine would be the unattainable. A sister—and he loved her with the love of a man!

It was the next day after the dream that they wandered again into the grove that sheltered Keith's old home, and again they entered it and went through the cold and empty rooms. In one of these rooms he sought among the titles of dusty rows of books until he came to one and opened it. And there he found what had been in the corner of his mind when the sun rose to give him courage after the night of his dream. The daughters of Achelous had lost in the end. Ulysses had tricked them. Ulysses had won. And in this day and age it was up to him, John Keith, to win, and win he would!

Always he felt this mastering certainty of the future when alone with Mary Josephine in the open day. With her at his side, her hand in his, and his arm about her waist, he told himself that all life was a lie—that there was no earth, no sun, no song or gladness in all the world, if that world held no hope for him. It was there. It was beyond the rim of forest. It was beyond the yellow plains, beyond the farthest timber of the farthest prairie, beyond the foothills; in the heart of the mountains was its abiding place. As he had dreamed of those mountains in boyhood and youth, so now he dreamed his dreams over again with Mary Josephine. For her he painted his pictures of them, as they wandered mile after mile up the shore of the Saskatchewan—the little world they would make all for themselves, how they would live, what they would do, the mysteries they would seek out, the triumphs they would achieve, the glory of that world—just for two. And Mary Josephine planned and dreamed with him.

In a week they lived what might have been encompassed in a year. So it seemed to Keith, who had known her only so long. With Mary Josephine the view-point was different. There had been a long separation, a separation filled with a heartbreak which she would never forget, but it had not served to weaken the bonds between her and this loved one, who, she thought, had always been her own. To her their comradeship was more complete now than it ever had been, even back in the old days, for they were alone in a land that was strange to her, and one was all that the world held for the other. So her possessorship of Keith was a thing which—again in the dark and brooding hours of night—sometimes made him writhe in an agony of shame. Hers was a shameless love, a love which had not even the lover's reason for embarrassment, a love unreserved and open as the day. It was her trick, nights, to nestle herself in the big armchair with him, and it was her fun to smother his face in her hair and tumble it about him, piling it over his mouth and nose until she made him plead for air. Again she would fit herself comfortably in the hollow of his arm and sit the evening out with her head on his shoulder, while they planned their future, and twice in that week she fell asleep there. Each morning she greeted him with a kiss, and each night she came to him to be kissed, and when it was her pleasure she kissed him—or made him kiss her—when they were on their long walks. It was bitter-sweet to Keith, and more frequently came the hours of crushing desolation for him, those hours in the still, dark night when his hypocrisy and his crime stood out stark and hideous in his troubled brain.

As this thing grew in him, a black and foreboding thunderstorm on the horizon of his dreams, an impulse which he did not resist dragged him more and more frequently down to the old home, and Mary Josephine was always with him. They let no one know of these visits. And they talked about John Keith, and in Mary Josephine's eyes he saw more than once a soft and starry glow of understanding. She loved the memory of this man because he, her brother, had loved him. And after these hours came the nights when truth, smiling at him, flung aside its mask and stood a grinning specter, and he measured to the depths the falseness of his triumph. His comfort was the thought that she knew. Whatever happened, she would know what John Keith had been. For he, John Keith, had told her. So much of the truth had he lived.

He fought against the new strain that was descending upon him slowly and steadily as the days passed. He could not but see the new light that had grown in Miriam Kirkstone's eyes. At times it was more than a dawn of hope. It was almost certainty. She had faith in him, faith in his promise to her, in his power to fight, his strength to win. Her growing friendship with Mary Josephine accentuated this, inspiring her at times almost to a point of conviction, for Mary Josephine's confidence in him was a passion. Even McDowell, primarily a fighter of his own battles, cautious and suspicious, had faith in him while he waited for Shan Tung. It was this blind belief in him that depressed him more than all else, for he knew that victory for himself must be based more or less on deceit and treachery. For the first time he heard Miriam laugh with Mary Josephine; he saw the gold and the brown head together out in the sun; he saw her face shining with a light that he had never seen there before, and then, when he came upon them, their faces were turned to him, and his heart bled even as he smiled and held out his hands to Mary Josephine. They trusted him, and he was a liar, a hypocrite, a Pharisee.

On the ninth day he had finished supper with Mary Josephine when the telephone rang. He rose to answer it. It was Miriam Kirkstone.

"He has returned," she said.

That was all. The words were in a choking voice. He answered and hung up the receiver. He knew a change had come into his face when he turned to Mary Josephine. He steeled himself to a composure that drew a questioning tenseness into her face. Gently he stroked her soft hair, explaining that Shan Tung had returned and that he was going to see him. In his bedroom he strapped his Service automatic under his coat.

At the door, ready to go, he paused. Mary Josephine came to him and put her hands to his shoulders. A strange unrest was in her eyes, a question which she did not ask.

Something whispered to him that it was the last time. Whatever happened now, tonight must leave him clean. His arms went around her, he drew her close against his breast, and for a space he held her there, looking into her eyes.

"You love me?" he asked softly.

"More than anything else in the world," she whispered.

105

"Kiss me, Mary Josephine."

Her lips pressed to his.

He released her from his arms, slowly, lingeringly.

After that she stood in the lighted doorway, watching him, until he disappeared in the gloom of the slope. She called good-by, and he answered her. The door closed.

And he went down into the valley, a hand of foreboding gripping at his heart.

CHAPTER 20

With a face out of which all color had fled, and eyes filled with the ghosts of a new horror, Miriam Kirkstone stood before Keith in the big room in the house on the hill.

"He was here—ten minutes," she said, and her voice was as if she was forcing it out of a part of her that was dead and cold. It was lifeless, emotionless, a living voice and yet strange with the chill of death. "In those ten minutes he told me—that! If you fail—"

It was her throat that held him, fascinated him. White, slim, beautiful— her heart seemed pulsing there. And he could see that heart choke back the words she was about to speak.

"If I fail—" he repeated the words slowly after her, watching that white, beating throat.

"There is only the one thing left for me to do. You—you—understand?"

"Yes, I understand. Therefore I shall not fail."

He backed away from her toward the door, and still he could not take his eyes from the white throat with its beating heart. "I shall not fail," he repeated. "And when the telephone rings, you will be here—to answer?"

"Yes, here," she replied huskily.

He went out. Under his feet the gravelly path ran through a flood of moonlight. Over him the sky was agleam with stars. It was a white night, one of those wonderful gold-white nights in the land of the Saskatchewan. Under that sky the world was alive. The little city lay in a golden glimmer of lights. Out of it rose a murmur, a rippling stream of sound, the voice of its life, softened by the little valley between. Into it Keith descended. He passed men and women, laughing, talking, gay. He heard music. The main street was a moving throng. On a corner the Salvation Army, a young woman, a young man, a crippled boy, two young girls, and an old man, were singing "Nearer, My God, to Thee." Opposite the Board of Trade building on the edge of the river a street medicine-fakir had drawn a crowd to his wagon. To the beat of the Salvation Army's tambourine rose the thrum of a made-up negro's banjo.

Through these things Keith passed, his eyes open, his ears listening, but he passed swiftly. What he saw and what he heard pressed upon him with the chilling thrill of that last swan-song, the swan-song of Ecla, of Kobat, of Ty, who had heard their doom chanted from the mountain-tops. It was the city rising up about his cars in rejoicing and triumph. And it put in his heart

107

a cold, impassive anger. He sensed an impending doom, and yet he was not afraid. He was no longer chained by dreams, no more restrained by self. Before his eyes, beating, beating, beating, he saw that tremulous heart in Miriam Kirkstone's soft, white throat.

He came to Shan Tung's. Beyond the softly curtained windows it was a yellow glare of light. He entered and met the flow of life, the murmur of voices and laughter, the tinkle of glasses, the scent of cigarette smoke, and the fainter perfume of incense. And where he had seen him last, as though he had not moved since that hour nine days ago, still with his cigarette, still sphinx-like, narrow-eyed, watchful, stood Li King.

Keith walked straight to him. And this time, as he approached, Li King greeted him with a quick and subtle smile. He nipped his cigarette to the tiled floor. He was bowing, gracious. Tonight he was not stupid.

"I have come to see Shan Tung," said Keith.

He had half expected to be refused, in which event he was prepared to use his prerogative as an officer of the law to gain his point. But Li King did not hesitate. He was almost eager. And Keith knew that Shan Tung was expecting him.

They passed behind one of the screens and then behind another, until it seemed to Keith their way was a sinuous twisting among screens. They paused before a panel in the wall, and Li King pressed the black throat of a long-legged, swan-necked bird with huge wings and the panel opened and swung toward them. It was dark inside, but Li King turned on a light. Through a narrow hallway ten feet in length he led the way, unlocked a second door, and held it open, smiling at Keith.

"Up there," he said.

A flight of steps led upward and as Keith began to mount them the door closed softly behind him. Li King accompanied him no further.

He mounted the steps, treading softly. At the top was another door, and this he opened as quietly as Li King had closed the one below him. Again the omnipresent screens, and then his eyes looked out upon a scene which made him pause in astonishment. It was a great room, a room fifty feet long by thirty in width, and never before had he beheld such luxury as it contained. His feet sank into velvet carpets, the walls were hung richly with the golds and browns and crimsons of priceless tapestries, and carven tables and divans of deep plush and oriental chairs filled the space before him. At the far end was a raised dais, and before this, illumined in candleglow, was a kneeling figure. He noticed then that there were many candles burning, that the room was lighted by candles, and that in their illumination the figure did not move. He caught the glint of armors standing up, warrior like, against the tapestries, and he wondered for a moment if the kneeling figure was a heathen god made of wood. It was then that he smelled the odor of frankincense; it crept subtly into his nostrils and his mouth, sweetened his breath, and made him cough.

At the far end, before the dais, the kneeling figure began to move. Its arms extended slowly, they swept backward, then out again, and three times the figure bowed itself and straightened, and with the movement came a low, human monotone. It was over quickly. Probably two full minutes had not passed since Keith had entered when the kneeling figure sprang to its feet with the quickness of a cat, faced about, and stood there, smiling and bowing and extending its hand.

"Good evening, John Keith!" It was Shan Tung. An oriental gown fell about him, draping him like a woman. It was a crimson gown, grotesquely ornamented with embroidered peacocks, and it flowed and swept about him in graceful undulations as he advanced, his footfalls making not the sound of a mouse on the velvet floors.

"Good evening, John Keith!" He was close, smiling, his eyes glowing, his hand still outstretched, friendliness in his voice and manner. And yet in that voice there was a purr, the purr of a cat watching its prey, and in his eyes a glow that was the soft rejoicing of a triumph.

Keith did not take the hand. He made as if he did not see it. He was looking into those glowing, confident eyes of the Chinaman. A Chinaman! Was it possible? Could a Chinaman possess that voice, whose very perfection shamed him?

Shan Tung seemed to read his thoughts. And what he found amused him, and he bowed again, still smiling. "I am Shan Tung," he said with the slightest inflection of irony. "Here—in my home—I am different. Do you not recognize me?"

He waved gracefully a hand toward a table on either side of which was a chair. He seated himself, not waiting for Keith. Keith sat down opposite him. Again he must have read what was in Keith's heart, the desire and the intent to kill, for suddenly he clapped his hands, not loudly, once—twice—

"You will join me in tea?" he asked.

Scarcely had he spoken when about them, on all sides of them it seemed to Keith, there was a rustle of life. He saw tapestries move. Before his eyes a panel became a door. There was a clicking, a stir as of gowns, soft footsteps, a movement in the air. Out of the panel doorway came a Chinaman with a cloth, napkins, and chinaware. Behind him followed a second with tea-urn and a bowl, and with the suddenness of an apparition, without sound or movement, a third was standing at Keith's side. And still there was rustling behind, still there was the whispering beat of life, and Keith knew that there were others. He did not flinch, but smiled back at Shan Tung. A minute, no more, and the soft-footed yellow men had performed their errands and were gone.

"Quick service," he acknowledged. "VERY quick service. Shan Tung! But I have my hand on something that is quicker!"

Suddenly Shan Tung leaned over the table. "John Keith, you are a fool if you came here with murder in your heart," he said. "Let us be friends. It is best. Let us be friends."

CHAPTER 21

It was as if with a swiftness invisible to the eye a mask had dropped from Shan Tung's face. Keith, preparing to fight, urging himself on to the step which he believed he must take, was amazed. Shan Tung was earnest. There was more than earnestness in his eyes, an anxiety, a frankly revealed hope that Keith would meet him halfway. But he did not offer his hand again. He seemed to sense, in that instant, the vast gulf between yellow and white. He felt Keith's contempt, the spurning contumely that was in the other's mind. Under the pallid texture of his skin there began to burn a slow and growing flush.

"Wait!" he said softly. In his flowing gown he seemed to glide to a carven desk near at hand. He was back in a moment with a roll of parchment in his hand. He sat down again and met Keith's eyes squarely and in silence for a moment.

"We are both MEN, John Keith." His voice was soft and calm. His tapering fingers with their carefully manicured nails fondled the roll of parchment, and then unrolled it, and held it so the other could read.

It was a university diploma. Keith stared. A strange name was scrolled upon it, Kao Lung, Prince of Shantung. His mind leaped to the truth. He looked at the other.

The man he had known as Shan Tung met his eyes with a quiet, strange smile, a smile in which there was pride, a flash of sovereignty, of a thing greater than skins that were white. "I am Prince Kao," he said. "That is my diploma. I am a graduate of Yale."

Keith's effort to speak was merely a grunt. He could find no words. And Kao, rolling up the parchment and forgetting the urn of tea that was growing cold, leaned a little over the table again. And then it was, deep in his narrowed, smoldering eyes, that Keith saw a devil, a living, burning thing of passion, Kao's soul itself. And Kao's voice was quiet, deadly.

"I recognized you in McDowell's office," he said. "I saw, first, that you were not Derwent Conniston. And then it was easy, so easy. Perhaps you killed Conniston. I am not asking, for I hated Conniston. Some day I should have killed him, if he had come back. John Keith, from that first time we met, you were a dead man. Why didn't I turn you over to the hangman? Why did I warn you in such a way that I knew you would come to see me? Why did I save your life which was in the hollow of my hand? Can you guess?"

111

"Partly," replied Keith. "But go on. I am waiting." Not for an instant had it enter his mind to deny that he was John Keith. Denial was folly, a waste of time, and just now he felt that nothing in the world was more precious to him than time.

Kao's quick mind, scheming and treacherous though it was, caught his view-point, and he nodded appreciatively. "Good, John Keith. It is easily guessed. Your life is mine. I can save it. I can destroy it. And you, in turn, can be of service to me. You help me, and I save you. It is a profitable arrangement. And we both are happy, for you keep Derwent Conniston's sister—and I—I get my golden-headed goddess, Miriam Kirkstone!"

"That much I have guessed," said Keith. "Go on!" For a moment Kao seemed to hesitate, to study the cold, gray passiveness of the other's face. "You love Derwent Conniston's sister," he continued in a voice still lower and softer. "And I—I love my golden-headed goddess. See! Up there on the dais I have her picture and a tress of her golden hair, and I worship them."

Colder and grayer was Keith's face as he saw the slumbering passion burn fiercer in Kao's eyes. It turned him sick. It was a terrible thing which could not be called love. It was a madness. But Kao, the man himself, was not mad. He was a monster. And while the eyes burned like two devils, his voice was still soft and low.

"I know what you are thinking; I see what you are seeing," he said. "You are thinking yellow, and you are seeing yellow. My skin! My birthright! My—" He smiled, and his voice was almost caressing.

"John Keith, in Pe-Chi-Li is the great city of Pekin, and Pe-Chi-Li is the greatest province in all China. And second only to that is the province of Shantung, which borders Pe-Chi-Li, the home of our Emperors for more centuries than you have years. And for so many generations that we cannot remember my forefathers have been rulers of Shantung. My grandfather was a Mandarin with the insignia of the Eighth Order, and my father was Ninth and highest of all Orders, with his palace at Tsi-Nan, on the Yellow Sea. And I, Prince Kao, eldest of his sons, came to America to learn American law and American ways. And I learned them, John Keith. I returned, and with my knowledge I undermined a government. For a time I was in power, and then this thing you call the god of luck turned against me, and I fled for my life. But the blood is still here—" he put his hand softly to his breast, "—the blood of a hundred generations of rulers. I tell you this because you dare not betray me, you dare not tell them who I am, though even that truth could not harm me. I prefer to be known as Shan Tung. Only you—and Miriam Kirkstone—have heard as much."

Keith's blood was like fire, but his voice was cold as ice. "GO ON!"

This time there could be no mistake. That cold gray of his passionless face, the steely glitter in his eyes, were read correctly by Kao. His eyes narrowed. For the first time a dull flame leaped into his colorless cheeks.

"Ah, I told you this because I thought we would work together, friends," he cried. "But it is not so. You, like my golden-headed goddess, hate me! You hate me because of my yellow skin. You say to yourself that I have a yellow heart. And she hates me, and she says that—but she is mine, MINE!" He sprang suddenly to his feet and swept about him with his flowing arms. "See what I have prepared for her! It is here she will come, here she will live until I take her away. There, on that dais, she will give up her soul and her beautiful body to me—and you cannot help it, she cannot help it, all the world cannot help it—AND SHE IS COMING TO ME TONIGHT!"

"TONIGHT!" gasped John Keith.

He, too, leaped to his feet. His face was ghastly. And Kao, in his silken gown, was sweeping his arms about him.

"See! The candles are lighted for her. They are waiting. And tonight, when the town is asleep, she will come. AND IT IS YOU WHO WILL MAKE HER COME, JOHN KEITH!"

Facing the devils in Kao's eyes, within striking distance of a creature who was no longer a man but a monster, Keith marveled at the coolness that held him back.

"Yes, it is you who will at last give her soul and her beautiful body to me," he repeated. "Come. I will show you how—and why!"

He glided toward the dais. His hand touched a panel. It opened and in the opening he turned about and waited for Keith.

"Come!" he said.

Keith, drawing a deep breath, his soul ready for the shock, his body ready for action, followed him.

CHAPTER 22

Into a narrow corridor, through a second door that seemed made of padded wool, and then into a dimly lighted room John Keith followed Kao, the Chinaman. Out of this room there was no other exit; it was almost square, its ceiling was low, its walls darkly somber, and that life was there Keith knew by the heaviness of cigarette smoke in the air. For a moment his eyes did not discern the physical evidence of that life. And then, staring at him out of the yellow glow, he saw a face. It was a haunting, terrible face, a face heavy and deeply lined by sagging flesh and with eyes sunken and staring. They were more than staring. They greeted Keith like living coals. Under the face was a human form, a big, fat, sagging form that leaned outward from its seat in a chair.

Kao, bowing, sweeping his flowing raiment with his arms, said, "John Keith, allow me to introduce you to Peter Kirkstone."

For the first time amazement, shock, came to Keith's lips in an audible cry. He advanced a step. Yes, in that pitiable wreck of a man he recognized Peter Kirkstone, the fat creature who had stood under the picture of the Madonna that fateful night, Miriam Kirkstone's brother!

And as he stood, speechless, Kao said: "Peter Kirkstone, you know why I have brought this man to you tonight. You know that he is not Derwent Conniston. You know that he is John Keith, the murderer of your father. Is it not so?"

The thick lips moved. The voice was husky—"Yes."

"He does not believe. So I have brought him that he may listen to you. Peter Kirkstone, is it your desire that your sister, Miriam, give herself to me, Prince Kao, tonight?"

Again the thick lips moved. This time Keith saw the effort. He shuddered. He knew these questions and answers had been prepared. A doomed man was speaking.

And the voice came, choking, "Yes."

"WHY?"

The terrible face of Peter Kirkstone seemed to contort. He looked at Kao. And Kao's eyes were shining in that dull room like the eyes of a snake.

"Because—it will save my life."

"And why will it save your life?"

Again that pause, again the sickly, choking effort. "Because—I HAVE KILLED A MAN."

Bowing, smiling, rustling, Kao turned to the door. "That is all, Peter Kirkstone. Good night. John Keith, will you follow me?"

Dumbly Keith followed through the dark corridor, into the big room mellow with candle-glow, back to the table with its mocking tea-urn and chinaware. He felt a thing like clammy sweat on his back. He sat down. And Kao sat opposite him again.

"That is the reason, John Keith. Peter Kirkstone, her brother, is a murderer, a cold-blooded murderer. And only Miriam Kirkstone and your humble servant, Prince Kao, know his secret. And to buy my secret, to save his life, the golden-headed goddess is almost ready to give herself to me— almost, John Keith. She will decide tonight, when you go to her. She will come. Yes, she will come tonight. I do not fear. I have prepared for her the candles, the bridal dais, the nuptial supper. Oh, she will come. For if she does not, if she fails, with tomorrow's dawn Peter Kirkstone and John Keith both go to the hangman!"

Keith, in spite of the horror that had come over him, felt no excitement. The whole situation was clear to him now, and there was nothing to be gained by argument, no possibility of evasion. Kao held the winning hand, the hand that put him back to the wall in the face of impossible alternatives. These alternatives flashed upon him swiftly. There were two and only two—flight, and alone, without Mary Josephine; and betrayal of Miriam Kirkstone. Just how Kao schemed that he should accomplish that betrayal, he could not guess.

His voice, like his face, was cold and strange when it answered the Chinaman; it lacked passion; there was no emphasis, no inflection that gave to one word more than to another. And Keith, listening to his own voice, knew what it meant. He was cold inside, cold as ice, and his eyes were on the dais, the sacrificial altar that Kao had prepared, waiting in the candleglow. On the floor of that dais was a great splash of dull-gold altar cloth, and it made him think of Miriam Kirkstone's unbound and disheveled hair strewn in its outraged glory over the thing Kao had prepared for her.

"I see. It is a trade, Kao. You are offering me my life in return for Miriam Kirkstone."

"More than that, John Keith. Mine is the small price. And yet it is great to me, for it gives me the golden goddess. But is she more to me than Derwent Conniston's sister may be to you? Yes, I am giving you her, and I am giving you your life, and I am giving Peter Kirkstone his life—all for ONE."

"For one," repeated Keith.

"Yes, for one."

"And I, John Keith, in some mysterious way unknown to me at present, am to deliver Miriam Kirkstone to you?"

"Yes."

"And yet, if I should kill you, now—where you sit—"

Kao shrugged his slim shoulders, and Keith heard that soft, gurgling laugh that McDowell had said was like the splutter of oil.

"I have arranged. It is all in writing. If anything should happen to me, there are messengers who would carry it swiftly. To harm me would be to seal your own doom. Besides, you would not leave here alive. I am not afraid."

"How am I to deliver Miriam Kirkstone to you?"

Kao leaned forward, his fingers interlacing eagerly. "Ah, NOW you have asked the question, John Keith! And we shall be friends, great friends, for you see with the eyes of wisdom. It will be easy, so easy that you will wonder at the cheapness of the task. Ten days ago Miriam Kirkstone was about to pay my price. And then you came. From that moment she saw you in McDowell's office, there was a sudden change. Why? I don't know. Perhaps because of that thing you call intuition but to which we give a greater name. Perhaps only because you were the man who had run down her father's murderer. I saw her that afternoon, before you went up at night. Ah, yes, I could see, I could understand the spark that had begun to grow in her, hope, a wild, impossible hope, and I prepared for it by leaving you my message. I went away. I knew that in a few days all that hope would be centered in you, that it would live and die in you, that in the end it would be your word that would bring her to me. And that word you must speak tonight. You must go to her, hope-broken. You must tell her that no power on earth can save her, and that Kao waits to make her a princess, that tomorrow will be too late, that TONIGHT must the bargain be closed. She will come. She will save her brother from the hangman, and you, in bringing her, will save John Keith and keep Derwent Conniston's sister. Is it not a great reward for the little I am asking?"

It was Keith who now smiled into the eyes of the Chinaman, but it was a smile that did not soften that gray and rock-like hardness that had settled in his face. "Kao, you are a devil. I suppose that is a compliment to your dirty ears. You're rotten to the core of the thing that beats in you like a heart;

you're a yellow snake from the skin in. I came to see you because I thought there might be a way out of this mess. I had almost made up my mind to kill you. But I won't do that. There's a better way. In half an hour I'll be with McDowell, and I'll beat you out by telling him that I'm John Keith. And I'll tell him this story of Miriam Kirkstone from beginning to end. I'll tell him of that dais you've built for her—your sacrificial altar!—and tomorrow Prince Albert will rise to a man to drag you out of this hole and kill you as they would kill a rat. That is my answer, you slit-eyed, Yale-veneered yellow devil! I may die, and Peter Kirkstone may die, but you'll not get Miriam Kirkstone!"

He was on his feet when he finished, amazed at the calmness of his own voice, amazed that his hands were steady and his brain was cool in this hour of his sacrifice. And Kao was stunned. Before his eyes he saw a white man throwing away his life. Here, in the final play, was a master-stroke he had not foreseen. A moment before the victor, he was now the vanquished. About him he saw his world falling, his power gone, his own life suddenly hanging by a thread. In Keith's face he read the truth. This white man was not bluffing. He would go to McDowell. He would tell the truth. This man who had ventured so much for his own life and freedom would now sacrifice that life to save a girl, one girl! He could not understand, and yet he believed. For it was there before his eyes in that gray, passionless face that was as inexorable as the face of one of his own stone gods.

As he uttered the words that smashed all that Kao had planned for, Keith sensed rather than saw the swift change of emotion sweeping through the yellow-visaged Moloch staring up at him. For a space the oriental's evil eyes had widened, exposing wider rims of saffron white, betraying his amazement, the shock of Keith's unexpected revolt, and then the lids closed slowly, until only dark and menacing gleams of fire shot between them, and Keith thought of the eyes of a snake. Swift as the strike of a rattler Kao was on his feet, his gown thrown back, one clawing hand jerking a derringer from his silken belt. In the same breath he raised his voice in a sharp call.

Keith sprang back. The snake-like threat in the Chinaman's eyes had prepared him, and his Service automatic leaped from its holster with lightning swiftness. Yet that movement was no swifter than the response to Kao's cry. The panel shot open, the screens moved, tapestries billowed suddenly as if moved by the wind, and Kao's servants sprang forth and were at him like a pack of dogs. Keith had no time to judge their number, for his brain was centered in the race with Kao's derringer. He saw its silver mountings flash in the candle-glow, saw its spurt of smoke and fire. But its report was drowned in the roar of his automatic as it replied with a stream of lead and flame. He saw the derringer fall and Kao crumple up like a jackknife. His brain turned red as he swung his weapon on the others, and as he fired, he backed toward the door. Then something caught him from behind, twisting his head almost from his shoulders, and he went down.

He lost his automatic. Weight of bodies was upon him; yellow hands clutched for his throat; he felt hot breaths and heard throaty cries. A madness of horror possessed him, a horror that was like the blind madness of Laocoon struggling with his sons in the coils of the giant serpent. In these moments he was not fighting men. They were monsters, yellow, foul-smelling, unhuman, and he fought as Laocoon fought. As if it had been a cane, he snapped the bone of an arm whose hand was throttling him; he twisted back a head until it snapped between its shoulders; he struck and broke with a blind fury and a giant strength, until at last, torn and covered with blood, he leaped free and reached the door. As he opened it and sprang through, he had the visual impression that only two of his assailants were rising from the floor.

For the space of a second he hesitated in the little hallway. Down the stairs was light—and people. He knew that he was bleeding and his clothes were torn, and that flight in that direction was impossible. At the opposite end of the hall was a curtain which he judged must cover a window. With a swift movement he tore down this curtain and found that he was right. In another second he had crashed the window outward with his shoulder, and felt the cool air of the night in his face. The door behind him was still closed when he crawled out upon a narrow landing at the top of a flight of steps leading down into the alley. He paused long enough to convince himself that his enemies were making no effort to follow him, and as he went down the steps, he caught himself grimly chuckling. He had given them enough.

In the darkness of the alley he paused again. A cool breeze fanned his cheeks, and the effect of it was to free him of the horror that had gripped him in his fight with the yellow men. Again the calmness with which he had faced Kao possessed him. The Chinaman was dead. He was sure of that. And for him there was not a minute to lose.

After all, it was his fate. The game had been played, and he had lost. There was one thing left undone, one play Conniston would still make, if he were there. And he, too, would make it. It was no longer necessary for him to give himself up to McDowell, for Kao was dead, and Miriam Kirkstone was saved. It was still right and just for him to fight for his life. But Mary

Josephine must know FROM HIM. It was the last square play he could make.

No one saw him as he made his way through alleys to the outskirts of the town. A quarter of an hour later he came up the slope to the Shack. It was lighted, and the curtains were raised to brighten his way up the hill. Mary Josephine was waiting for him.

Again there came over him the strange and deadly calmness with which he had met the tragedy of that night. He had tried to wipe the blood from his face, but it was still there when he entered and faced Mary Josephine. The wounds made by the razor-like nails of his assailants were bleeding; he was hatless, his hair was disheveled, and his throat and a part of his chest were bare where his clothes had been torn away. As Mary Josephine came toward him, her arms reaching out to him, her face dead white, he stretched out a restraining hand, and said,

"Please wait, Mary Josephine!"

Something stopped her—the strangeness of his voice, the terrible hardness of his face, gray and blood-stained, the something appalling and commanding in the way he had spoken. He passed her quickly on his way to the telephone. Her lips moved; she tried to speak; one of her hands went to her throat. He was calling Miriam Kirkstone's number! And now she saw that his hands, too, were bleeding. There came the murmur of a voice in the telephone. Someone answered. And then she heard him say,

"SHAN TUNG IS DEAD!"

That was all. He hung up the receiver and turned toward her. With a little cry she moved toward him.

"DERRY—DERRY—"

He evaded her and pointed to the big chair in front of the fireplace. "Sit down, Mary Josephine."

She obeyed him. Her face was whiter than he had thought a living face could be, And then, from the beginning to the end, he told her everything. Mary Josephine made no sound, and in the big chair she seemed to crumple smaller and smaller as he confessed the great lie to her, from the hour Conniston and he had traded identities in the little cabin on the Barren. Until he died he knew she would haunt him as he saw her there for the last time—her dead-white face, her great eyes, her voiceless lips, her two little hands clutched at her breast as she listened to the story of the great lie and his love for her.

119

Even when he had done, she did not move or speak. He went into his room, closed the door, and turned on the lights. Quickly he put into his pack what he needed. And when he was ready, he wrote on a piece of paper:

"A thousand times I repeat, 'I love you.' Forgive me if you can. If you cannot forgive, you may tell McDowell, and the Law will find me up at the place of our dreams—the river's end.

—John Keith."

This last message he left on the table for Mary Josephine.

For a moment he listened at the door. Outside there was no movement, no sound. Quietly, then, he raised the window through which Kao had come into his room.

A moment later he stood under the light of the brilliant stars. Faintly there came to him the sounds of the city, the sound of life, of gayety, of laughter and of happiness, rising to him now from out of the valley.

He faced the north. Down the side of the hill and over the valley lay the forests. And through the starlight he strode back to them once more, back to their cloisters and their heritage, the heritage of the hunted and the outcast.

CHAPTER 23

All through the starlit hours of that night John Keith trudged steadily into the Northwest. For a long time his direction took him through slashings, second-growth timber, and cleared lands; he followed rough roads and worn trails and passed cabins that were dark and without life in the silence of midnight. Twice a dog caught the stranger scent in the air and howled; once he heard a man's voice, far away, raised in a shout. Then the trails grew rougher. He came to a deep wide swamp. He remembered that swamp, and before he plunged into it, he struck a match to look at his compass and his watch. It took him two hours to make the other side. He was in the deep and uncut timber then, and a sense of relief swept over him.

The forest was again his only friend. He did not rest. His brain and his body demanded the action of steady progress, though it was not through fear of what lay behind him. Fear had ceased to be a stimulating part of him; it was even dead within him. It was as if his energy was engaged in fighting for a principle, and the principle was his life; he was following a duty, and this duty impelled him to make his greatest effort. He saw clearly what he had done and what was ahead of him. He was twice a killer of men now, and each time the killing had rid the earth of a snake. This last time it had been an exceedingly good job. Even McDowell would concede that, and Miriam Kirkstone, on her knees, would thank God for what he had done. But Canadian law did not split hairs like its big neighbor on the south. It wanted him at least for Kirkstone's killing if not for that of Kao, the Chinaman. No one, not even Mary Josephine, would ever fully realize what he had sacrificed for the daughter of the man who had ruined his father. For Mary Josephine would never understand how deeply he had loved her.

It surprised him to find how naturally he fell back into his old habit of discussing things with himself, and how completely and calmly he accepted the fact that his home-coming had been but a brief and wonderful interlude to his fugitivism. He did not know it at first, but this calmness was the calmness of a despair more fatal than the menace of the hangman.

"They won't catch me," he encouraged himself. "And she won't tell them where I'm going. No, she won't do that." He found himself repeating that thought over and over again. Mary Josephine would not betray him. He repeated it, not as a conviction, but to fight back and hold down another thought that persisted in forcing itself upon him. And this thing, that at times was like a voice within him, cried out in its moments of life, "She hates you—and she WILL tell where you are going!"

With each hour it was harder for him to keep that voice down; it persisted, it grew stronger; in its intervals of triumph it rose over and submerged all other thoughts in him. It was not his fear of her betrayal that stabbed him; it was the underlying motive of it, the hatred that would inspire it. He tried not to vision her as he had seen her last, in the big chair, crushed, shamed, outraged—seeing in him no longer the beloved brother, but an impostor, a criminal, a man whom she might suspect of killing that brother for his name and his place in life. But the thing forced itself on him. It was reasonable, and it was justice.

"But she won't do it," he told himself. "She won't do it."

This was his fight, and its winning meant more to him than freedom. It was Mary Josephine who would live with him now, and not Conniston. It was her spirit that would abide with him, her voice he would hear in the whispers of the night, her face he would see in the glow of his lonely fires, and she must remain with him always as the Mary Josephine he had known. So he crushed back the whispering voice, beat it down with his hands clenched at his side, fought it through the hours of that night with the desperation of one who fights for a thing greater than life.

Toward dawn the stars began to fade out of the sky. He had been tireless, and he was tireless now. He felt no exhaustion. Through the gray gloom that came before day he went on, and the first glow of sun found him still traveling. Prince Albert and the Saskatchewan were thirty miles to the south and east of him.

He stopped at last on the edge of a little lake and unburdened himself of his pack for the first time. He was glad that the premonition of just such a sudden flight as this had urged him to fill his emergency grub-sack yesterday morning. "Won't do any harm for us to be prepared," he had laughed jokingly to Mary Josephine, and Mary Josephine herself had made him double the portion of bacon because she was fond of it. It was hard for him to slice that bacon without a lump rising in his throat. Pork and love! He wanted to laugh, and he wanted to cry, and between the two it was a queer, half-choked sound that came to his lips. He ate a good breakfast, rested for a couple of hours, and went on. At a more leisurely pace he traveled through most of the day, and at night he camped. In the ten days following his flight from Prince Albert he kept utterly out of sight. He avoided trappers' shacks and trails and occasional Indians. He rid himself of his beard and shaved himself every other day. Mary Josephine had never cared much for the beard. It prickled. She had wanted him smooth-faced, and now he was that. He looked better, too. But the most striking resemblance to Derwent Conniston was gone. At the end of the ten days he was at Turtle Lake, fifty miles east of Fort Pitt. He believed that he could show himself openly now, and on the tenth day bartered with some Indians for fresh supplies. Then he struck south of Fort Pitt, crossed the Saskatchewan, and hit between the Blackfoot Hills and the Vermillion River into the Buffalo Coulee country. In the open country he came upon occasional ranches, and at one of these he purchased a pack-horse. At Buffalo Lake he bought his supplies for the mountains, including fifty steel traps, crossed the upper branch of the Canadian Pacific at night, and the next day saw in the far distance the purple haze of the Rockies.

It was six weeks after the night in Kao's place that he struck the Saskatchewan again above the Brazeau. He did not hurry now. Just ahead of him slumbered the mountains; very close was the place of his dreams. But he was no longer impelled by the mighty lure of the years that were gone. Day by day something had worn away that lure, as the ceaseless grind of water wears away rock, and for two weeks he wandered slowly and without purpose in the green valleys that lay under the snow-tipped peaks of the ranges. He was gripped in the agony of an unutterable loneliness, which fell upon and scourged him like a disease. It was a deeper and more bitter thing than a yearning for companionship. He might have found that. Twice he was near camps. Three times he saw outfits coming out, and purposely drew away from them. He had no desire to meet men, no desire to talk or to be troubled by talking. Day And night his body and his soul cried out for Mary Josephine, and in his despair he cursed those who had taken her away from him. It was a crisis which was bound to come, and in his aloneness he fought it out. Day after day he fought it, until his face and his heart bore the scars of it. It was as if a being on whom he had set all his worship had died, only it was worse than death. Dead, Mary Josephine would still have been his inspiration; in a way she would have belonged to him. But living, hating him as she must, his dreams of her were a sacrilege and his love for her like the cut of a sword. In the end he was like a man who had triumphed over a malady that would always leave its marks upon him. In the beginning of the third week he knew that he had conquered, just as he had triumphed in a similar way over death and despair in the north. He would go into the mountains, as he had planned. He would build his cabin. And if the Law came to get him, it was possible that again he would fight.

On the second day of this third week he saw advancing toward him a solitary horseman. The stranger was possibly a mile away when he discovered him, and he was coming straight down the flat of the valley. That he was not accompanied by a pack-horse surprised Keith, for he was bound out of the mountains and not in. Then it occurred to him that he might be a prospector whose supplies were exhausted, and that he was easing his journey by using his pack as a mount. Whoever and whatever he was, Keith was not in any humor to meet him, and without attempting to conceal himself he swung away from the river, as if to climb the slope of the mountain on his right. No sooner had he clearly signified the new direction he was taking, than the stranger deliberately altered his course in a way to cut him off. Keith was irritated. Climbing up a narrow terrace of shale, he headed straight up the slope, as if his intention were to reach the higher terraces of the mountain, and then he swung suddenly down into a coulee, where he was out of sight. Here he waited for ten minutes, then struck deliberately and openly back into the valley. He chuckled when he saw how cleverly his ruse had worked. The stranger was a quarter of a mile up the mountain and still climbing.

"Now what the devil is he taking all that trouble for?" Keith asked himself.

An instant later the stranger saw him again. For perhaps a minute he halted, and in that minute Keith fancied he was getting a round cursing. Then the stranger headed for him, and this time there was no escape, for the moment he struck the shelving slope of the valley, he prodded his horse into a canter, swiftly diminishing the distance between them. Keith unbuttoned the flap of his pistol holster and maneuvered so that he would be partly concealed by his pack when the horseman rode up. The persistence of the stranger suggested to him that Mary Josephine had lost no time in telling McDowell where the law would be most likely to find him.

Then he looked over the neck of his pack at the horseman, who was quite near, and was convinced that he was not an officer. He was still jogging at a canter and riding atrociously. One leg was napping as if it had lost its stirrup-hold; the rider's arms were pumping, and his hat was sailing behind at the end of a string.

"Whoa!" said Keith.

His heart stopped its action. He was staring at a big red beard and a huge, shaggy head. The horseman reined in, floundered from his saddle, and swayed forward as if seasick.

"Well, I'll be—"

124

"DUGGAN!"
"JOHNNY—JOHNNY KEITH!"

CHAPTER 24

For a matter of ten seconds neither of the two men moved. Keith was stunned. Andy Duggan's eyes were fairly popping out from under his bushy brows. And then unmistakably Keith caught the scent of bacon in the air.

"Andy—Andy Duggan," he choked. "You know me—you know Johnny Keith—you know me—you—"

Duggan answered with an inarticulate bellow and jumped at Keith as if to bear him to the ground. He hugged him, and Keith hugged, and then for a minute they stood pumping hands until their faces were red, and Duggan was growling over and over:

"An' you passed me there at McCoffin's Bend—an' I didn't know you, I didn't know you, I didn't know you! I thought you was that cussed Conniston! I did. I thought you was Conniston!" He stood back at last. "Johnny—Johnny Keith!"

"Andy, you blessed old devil!"

They pumped hands again, pounded shoulders until they were sore, and in Keith's face blazed once more the love of life.

Suddenly old Duggan grew rigid and sniffed the air. "I smell bacon!"

"It's in the pack, Andy. But for Heaven's sake don't notice the bacon until you explain how you happen to be here."

"Been waitin' for you," replied Duggan in an affectionate growl. "Knew you'd have to come down this valley to hit the Little Fork. Been waitin' six weeks."

Keith dug his fingers into Duggan's arm.

"How did you know I was coming HERE?" he demanded. "Who told you?"

"All come out in the wash, Johnny. Pretty mess. Chinaman dead. Johnny Keith, alias Conniston, alive an' living with Conniston's pretty sister. Johnny gone—skipped. No one knew where. I made guesses. Knew the girl would know if anyone did. I went to her, told her how you'n me had been pals, an' she give me the idee you was goin' up to the river's end. I resigned from the Betty M., that night. Told her, though, that she was a ninny if she thought you'd go up there. Made her believe the note was just a blind."

"My God," breathed Keith hopelessly, "I meant it."

"Sure you did, Johnny. I knew it. But I didn't dare let HER know it. If you could ha' seen that pretty mouth o' hern curlin' up as if she'd liked to have bit open your throat, an' her hands clenched, an' that murder in her

126

eyes—Man, I lied to her then! I told her I was after you, an' that if she wouldn't put the police on you, I'd bring back your head to her, as they used to do in the old times. An' she bit. Yes, sir, she said to me, 'If you'll do that, I won't say a word to the police!' An' here I am, Johnny. An' if I keep my word with that little tiger, I've got to shoot you right now. Haw! Haw!"

Keith had turned his face away.

Duggan, pulling him about by the shoulders, opened his eyes wide in amazement.—"Johnny—"

"Maybe you don't understand, Andy," struggled Keith. "I'm sorry—she feels—like that."

For a moment Duggan was silent. Then he exploded with a sudden curse. "SORRY! What the devil you sorry for, Johnny? You treated her square, an' you left her almost all of Conniston's money. She ain't no kick comin', and she ain't no reason for feelin' like she does. Let 'er go to the devil, I say. She's pretty an' sweet an' all that—but when anybody wants to go clawin' your heart out, don't be fool enough to feel sorry about it. You lied to her, but what's that? There's bigger lies than yourn been told, Johnny, a whole sight bigger! Don't you go worryin'. I've been here waitin' six weeks, an' I've done a lot of thinkin', and all our plans are set an' hatched. An' I've got the nicest cabin all built and waitin' for us up the Little Fork. Here we are. Let's be joyful, son!" He laughed into Keith's tense, gray face. "Let's be joyful!"

Keith forced a grin. Duggan didn't know. He hadn't guessed what that "little tiger who would have liked to have bit open his throat" had been to him. The thick-headed old hero, loyal to the bottom of his soul, hadn't guessed. And it came to Keith then that he would never tell him. He would keep that secret. He would bury it in his burned-out soul, and he would be "joyful" if he could. Duggan's blazing, happy face, half buried in its great beard, was like the inspiration and cheer of a sun rising on a dark world. He was not alone. Duggan, the old Duggan of years ago, the Duggan who had planned and dreamed with him, his best friend, was with him now, and the light came back into his face as he looked toward the mountains. Off there, only a few miles distant, was the Little Fork, winding into the heart of the Rockies, seeking out its hidden valleys, its trailless canons, its hidden mysteries. Life lay ahead of him, life with its thrill and adventure, and at his side was the friend of all friends to seek it with him. He thrust out his hands.

"God bless you, Andy," he cried. "You're the gamest pal that ever lived!"

A moment later Duggan pointed to a clump of timber half a mile ahead. "It's past dinner-time," he said. "There's wood. If you've got any bacon aboard, I move we eat."

An hour later Andy was demonstrating that his appetite was as voracious as ever. Before describing more of his own activities, he insisted that Keith recite his adventures from the night "he killed that old skunk, Kirkstone."

It was two o'clock when they resumed their journey. An hour later they struck the Little Fork and until seven traveled up the stream. They were deep in the lap of the mountains when they camped for the night. After supper, smoking his pipe, Duggan stretched himself out comfortably with his back to a tree.

"Good thing you come along when you did, Johnny," he said. "I been waitin' in that valley ten days, an' the eats was about gone when you hove in sight. Meant to hike back to the cabin for supplies tomorrow or next day. Gawd, ain't this the life! An' we're goin' to find gold, Johnny, we're goin' to find it!"

"We've got all our lives to—to find it in," said Keith.

Duggan puffed out a huge cloud of smoke and heaved a great sigh of pleasure. Then he grunted and chuckled. "Lord, what a little firebrand that sister of Conniston's is!" he exclaimed. "Johnny, I bet if you'd walk in on her now, she'd kill you with her own hands. Don't see why she hates you so, just because you tried to save your life. Of course you must ha' lied like the devil. Couldn't help it. But a lie ain't nothin'. I've told some whoppers, an' no one ain't never wanted to kill me for it. I ain't afraid of McDowell. Everyone said the Chink was a good riddance. It's the girl. There won't be a minute all her life she ain't thinkin' of you, an' she won't be satisfied until she's got you. That is, she thinks she won't. But we'll fool the little devil, Johnny. We'll keep our eyes open—an' fool her!"

"Let's talk of pleasanter things," said Keith. "I've got fifty traps in the pack, Andy. You remember how we used to plan on trapping during the winter and hunting for gold during the summer?"

Duggan rubbed his hands until they made a rasping sound; he talked of lynx signs he had seen, and of marten and fox. He had panned "colors" at a dozen places along the Little Fork and was ready to make his affidavit that it was the same gold he had dredged at McCoffin's Bend.

"If we don't find it this fall, we'll be sittin' on the mother lode next summer," he declared, and from then until it was time to turn in he talked of nothing but the yellow treasure it had been his lifelong dream to find. At the last, when they had rolled in their blankets, he raised himself on his elbow for a moment and said to Keith:

"Johnny, don't you worry about that Conniston girl. I forgot to tell you I've took time by the forelock. Two weeks ago I wrote an' told her I'd learned you was hittin' into the Great Slave country, an' that I was about to hike after you. So go to sleep an' don't worry about that pesky little rattlesnake."

"I'm not worrying," said Keith.

Fifteen minutes later he heard Duggan snoring. Quietly he unwrapped his blanket and sat up. There were still burning embers in the fire, the night—like that first night of his flight—was a glory of stars, and the moon was rising. Their camp was in a small, meadowy pocket in the center of which was a shimmering little lake across which he could easily have thrown a stone. On the far side of this was the sheer wall of a mountain, and the top of this wall, thousands of feet up, caught the glow of the moon first. Without awakening his comrade, Keith walked to the lake. He watched the golden illumination as it fell swiftly lower over the face of the mountain. He could see it move like a great flood. And then, suddenly, his shadow shot out ahead of him, and he turned to find the moon itself glowing like a monstrous ball between the low shoulders of a mountain to the east. The world about him became all at once vividly and wildly beautiful. It was as if a curtain had lifted so swiftly the eye could not follow it. Every tree and shrub and rock stood out in a mellow spotlight; the lake was transformed to a pool of molten silver, and as far as he could see, where shoulders and ridges did not cut him out, the moonlight was playing on the mountains. In the air was a soft droning like low music, and from a distant crag came the rattle of loosened rocks. He fancied, for a moment, that Mary Josephine was standing at his side, and that together they were drinking in the wonder of this dream at last come true. Then a cry came to his lips, a broken, gasping man-cry which he could not keep back, and his heart was filled with anguish.

With all its beauty, all its splendor of quiet and peace, the night was a bitter one for Keith, the bitterest of his life. He had not believed the worst of Mary Josephine. He knew he had lost her and that she might despise him, but that she would actually hate him with the desire for a personal vengeance he had not believed. Was Duggan right? Was Mary Josephine unfair? And should he in self-defense fight to poison his own thoughts against her? His face set hard, and a joyless laugh fell from his lips. He knew that he was facing the inevitable. No matter what had happened, he must go on loving Mary Josephine.

All through that night he was awake. Half a dozen times he went to his blanket, but it was impossible for him to sleep. At four o'clock he built up the fire and at five roused Duggan. The old river-man sprang up with the enthusiasm of a boy. He came back from the lake with his beard and head dripping and his face glowing. All the mountains held no cheerier comrade than Duggan.

They were on the trail at six o'clock and hour after hour kept steadily up the Little Fork. The trail grew rougher, narrower, and more difficult to follow, and at intervals Duggan halted to make sure of the way. At one of these times he said to Keith:

"Las' night proved there ain't no danger from her, Johnny. I had a dream, an' dreams goes by contraries an' always have. What you dream never comes true. It's always the opposite. An' I dreamed that little she-devil come up on you when you was asleep, took a big bread-knife, an' cut your head plumb off! Yessir, I could see her holdin' up that head o' yourn, an' the blood was drippin', an' she was a-laughin'—"

"SHUT UP!" Keith fairly yelled the words. His eyes blazed. His face was dead white.

With a shrug of his huge shoulders and a sullen grunt Duggan went on.

An hour later the trail narrowed into a short canon, and this canon, to Keith's surprise, opened suddenly into a beautiful valley, a narrow oasis of green hugged in between the two ranges. Scarcely had they entered it, when Duggan raised his voice in a series of wild yells and began firing his rifle into the air.

"Home-coming," he explained to Keith, after he was done. "Cabin's just over that bulge. Be there in ten minutes."

In less than ten minutes Keith saw it, sheltered in the edge of a thick growth of cedar and spruce from which its timbers had been taken. It was a larger cabin than he had expected to see—twice, three times as large.

"How did you do it alone!" he exclaimed in admiration. "It's a wonder, Andy. Big enough for—for a whole family!"

"Half a dozen Indians happened along, an' I hired 'em," explained Duggan. "Thought I might as well make it big enough, Johnny, seein' I had plenty of help. Sometimes I snore pretty loud, an'—"

"There's smoke coming out of it," cried Keith.

"Kept one of the Indians," chuckled Duggan. "Fine cook, an' a sassy-lookin' little squaw she is, Johnny. Her husband died last winter, an' she jumped at the chance to stay, for her board an' five bucks a month. How's your Uncle Andy for a schemer, eh, Johnny?"

A dozen rods from the cabin was a creek. Duggan halted here to water his horse and nodded for Keith to go on.

"Take a look, Johnny; go ahead an' take a look! I'm sort of sot up over that cabin."

Keith handed his reins to Duggan and obeyed. The cabin door was open, and he entered. One look assured him that Duggan had good reason to be "sot up." The first big room reminded him of the Shack. Beyond that was another room in which he heard someone moving and the crackle of a fire in a stove. Outside Duggan was whistling. He broke off whistling to sing, and as Keith listened to the river-man's bellowing voice chanting the words of the song he had sung at McCoffin's Bend for twenty years, he grinned. And then he heard the humming of a voice in the kitchen. Even the squaw was happy.

And then—and then—

"GREAT GOD IN HEAVEN—"

In the doorway she stood, her arms reaching out to him, love, glory, triumph in her face—MARY JOSEPHINE!

He swayed; he groped out; something blinded him—tears—hot, blinding tears that choked him, that came with a sob in his throat. And then she was in his arms, and her arms were around him, and she was laughing and crying, and he heard her say: "Why—why didn't you come back—to me— that night? Why—why did you—go out—through the—window? I—I was waiting—and I—I'd have gone—with you—"

From the door behind them came Duggan's voice, chuckling, exultant, booming with triumph. "Johnny, didn't I tell you there was lots bigger lies than yourn? Didn't I? Eh?"

131

CHAPTER 25

It was many minutes, after Keith's arms had closed around Mary Josephine, before he released her enough to hold her out and look at her. She was there, every bit of her, eyes glowing with a greater glory and her face wildly aflush with a thing that had never been there before; and suddenly, as he devoured her in that hungry look, she gave a little cry, and hugged herself to his breast, and hid her face there.

And he was whispering again and again, as though he could find no other word,

"Mary—Mary—Mary—"

Duggan drew away from the door. The two had paid no attention to his voice, and the old river-man was one continuous chuckle as he unpacked Keith's horse and attended to his own, hobbling them both and tying cow-bells to them. It was half an hour before he ventured up out of the grove along the creek and approached the cabin again. Even then he halted, fussing with a piece of harness, until he saw Mary Josephine in the door. The sun was shining on her. Her glorious hair was down, and behind her was Keith, so close that his shoulders were covered with it. Like a bird Mary Josephine sped to Duggan. Great red beard and all she hugged him, and on the flaming red of his bare cheek-bone she kissed him.

"Gosh," said Duggan, at a loss for something better to say. "Gosh—"

Then Keith had him by the hand. "Andy, you ripsnorting old liar, if you weren't old enough to be my father, I'd whale the daylights out of you!" he cried joyously. "I would, just because I love you so! You've made this day the—the—the—"

"—The most memorable of my life," helped Mary Josephine. "Is that it—John?"

Timidly, for the first time, her cheek against his shoulder, she spoke his name. And before Duggan's eyes Keith kissed her.

Hours later, in a world aglow with the light of stars and a radiant moon, Keith and Mary Josephine were alone out in the heart of their little valley. To Keith it was last night returned, only more wonderful. There was the same droning song in the still air, the low rippling of running water, the mysterious whisperings of the mountains. All about them were the guardian peaks of the snow-capped ranges, and under their feet was the soft lush of grass and the sweet scent of flowers. "Our valley of dreams," Mary Josephine had named it, an infinite happiness trembling in her voice. "Our beautiful valley of dreams—come true!" "And you would have come with me—that night?" asked Keith wonderingly. "That night—I ran away?"

"Yes. I didn't hear you go. And at last I went to your door and listened, and then I knocked, and after that I called to you, and when you didn't answer, I entered your room."

"Dear heaven!" breathed Keith. "After all that, you would have come away with me, covered with blood, a—a murderer, they say—a hunted man—"

"John, dear." She took one of his hands in both her own and held it tight. "John, dear, I've got something to tell you."

He was silent.

"I made Duggan promise not to tell you I was here when he found you, and I made him promise something else—to keep a secret I wanted to tell you myself. It was wonderful of him. I don't see how he did it."

She snuggled still closer to him, and held his hand a little tighter. "You see, John, there was a terrible time after you killed Shan Tung. Only a little while after you had gone, I saw the sky growing red. It was Shan Tung's place—afire. I was terrified, and my heart was broken, and I didn't move. I must have sat at the window a long time, when the door burst open suddenly and Miriam ran in, and behind her came McDowell. Oh, I never heard a man swear as McDowell swore when he found you had gone, and Miriam flung herself on the floor at my feet and buried her head in my lap.

"McDowell tramped up and down, and at last he turned to me as if he was going to eat me, and he fairly shouted, 'Do you know—THAT CURSED FOOL DIDN'T KILL JUDGE KIRKSTONE!'"

There was a pause in which Keith's brain reeled. And Mary Josephine went on, as quietly as though she were talking about that evening's sunset:

"Of course, I knew all along, from what you had told me about John Keith, that he wasn't what you would call a murderer. You see, John, I had learned to LOVE John Keith. It was the other thing that horrified me! In the fight, that night, Judge Kirkstone wasn't badly hurt, just stunned. Peter Kirkstone and his father were always quarreling. Peter wanted money, and his father wouldn't give it to him. It seems impossible,—what happened then. But it's true. After you were gone, PETER KIRKSTONE KILLED HIS FATHER THAT HE MIGHT INHERIT THE ESTATE! And then he laid the crime on you!"

"My God!" breathed Keith. "Mary—Mary Josephine—how do you know?"

133

"Peter Kirkstone was terribly burned in the fire. He died that night, and before he died he confessed. That was the power Shan Tung held over Miriam. He knew. And Miriam was to pay the price that would save her brother from the hangman."

"And that," whispered Keith, as if to himself, "was why she was so interested in John Keith."

He looked away into the shimmering distance of the night, and for a long time both were silent. A woman had found happiness. A man's soul had come out of darkness into light.

THE END

CPSIA information can be obtained at www.ICGtesting.com
Printed in the USA
LVOW04s0612191214

419480LV00014B/159/P